Vince's Vixen

Heroes for Hire, Book 19

Dale Mayer

1- 805 639-9436

VINCE'S VIXEN: HEROES FOR HIRE, BOOK 19
Dale Mayer
Valley Publishing Ltd.

ISBN-13: 978-1-773361-26-0
Print Edition

Books in This Series:

About This Book

Running away can often lead to the same thing you were trying to leave behind ...

Vince is not on board with the wave of romance happening at Legendary Security and so is happy to escape all that, but he soon finds himself aboard a research vessel off the coast of the Galapagos Islands, dealing with his own tide of emotions.

Vanessa loves her research trips. This latest one is finally coming to a successful conclusion, as she completes their data collection, when their vessel is boarded by pirates. She's knocked unconscious and moved to an old sinking tub and left adrift in the ocean. She wakes to find the only other female member of the team is missing ...

Worried, the team returns to shore, trying to sort out what happened. Vanessa insists on tracking her missing team member, even as the others vote to return home. Vanessa refuses. She'll help or die trying. Vince can stay with her or go with the others—his choice—but no way is Vanessa's lost researcher being left behind.

And, one by one, the other members of the team go missing too ...

Prologue

ON HIS WAY to buy steaks for dinner, Vince Manor had been stopped with a phone call. As he stood in the compound, he heard Dezi and Diamond in a corner of the room.

He shook his head at Dezi. "Holy crap," he said, watching the two. He knew it was serious, but he hadn't realized just how serious.

Levi walked in to stand beside him and said, "You're next."

"That's guaranteed to make me run," Vince said. "This is freaking scary stuff."

"No," Levi said. "It's the best thing that can happen to any of us. Don't be scared of it. When it's your turn, you'll know it."

"Nah," Vince said, "everybody around me has all the good women. There isn't another one left in the world, I'm sure. Knowing me, I'll end up with some nutcase, a bitch, and I mean that in the nicest canine way."

Levi chuckled. "No, but maybe what you need is somebody with a bit of spirit, somebody to help you laugh."

"Oh, no," he said. "No matchmaking."

"No matchmaking required," Levi said. "I'm pretty sure the next job with your name on it will find you the perfect woman."

"Hell no. And, if her name starts with a *V*, I'm out of there. There will be no Victorias in my world or Valeries or Veras or anything else."

Levi chuckled, then burst into great big guffaws of laughter.

"What are you laughing at?" Vince asked suspiciously.

"I know exactly what it'll be. It'll be *Vince's Vixen.*" Then he went off in a storm of laughter again.

Vince stared at him. "Oh, hell no," he said. The last thing he wanted was somebody who would argue all the time. He wanted spirit, yes, but he sure as hell didn't want too much of it.

And he had a sad feeling it was just too damn bad. Levi had already forecasted Vince's future. Whether he liked it or not.

Chapter 1

T HE CRACKLING STATIC of the PA system shook Vince
out of the computer work he was doing. He was in the
office at the compound, handling some of the research he
took over for Stone so he could upgrade the security system.
With the advent of the completed swimming pool installa-
tion, they'd added in fences and made strategic use of plants
from California in the yard too, so now they were taking a
new look at security and who could see stuff going on in the
pool area.

Of course, Reyes and Raina were handling that part. It
was always about security here. And Vince understood that.
Often meetings were all about new ideas, new concepts they
were sorting out through research. He was currently looking
at a different kind of sensor to allow them to see if anybody
moved within one hundred yards of the perimeter of the
compound. The problem with that, given the countryside
they lived in, was the animal wildlife. Levi could put up a
sensor and set a target weight for detecting an intruder, so
anybody moving in the two-hundred-pound category would
set off the alarm, whereas anything small, like a coyote,
wouldn't. And, of course, that would help, but would it be
effective? And an awful lot of crazy-ass men were out there
who were in the 150-pound range. Women too...

Vince continued going through the research, printing off

and circling sections he thought should be reviewed.

"Full staff meeting in the kitchen right now please," said Ice, her voice coming across the PA system. "We have a call coming in. Attention, everyone. A team is going out immediately. All hands on deck."

Vince closed down what he was working on, stacked up the research paperwork and headed to the kitchen. Being on paperwork duty wasn't his ideal task. He understood the necessity, but, if there was an op, he wanted in on it.

He really enjoyed being here, loving the camaraderie of working for Levi and Ice. They were now engaged, with no wedding date planned yet, but Ice's face always held a smile. For that, Vince had to give it hands down to Levi. He'd done a good thing when he had asked her to marry him. Levi probably didn't know how much it meant to some people, and maybe Levi didn't even think it was important to Ice. She always seemed so independent and so capable. But then Levi must have realized how much their lives were entwined and that a commitment mattered to her.

And it had.

As Vince walked into the kitchen, a good seven people already waited. That was reassuring. His odds of going out on the job just went up. He frowned. "Not many are here, huh?"

Stone looked up. "Two headed out last night. We're down to a skeleton crew. Instead of wondering when we'll have some work, we're in a constant state of not having enough men." He wore a hard smile. "The world is in a sucky spot right now."

"Isn't that the truth." Vince headed to the sideboard, poured himself a fresh cup of coffee, grinned when he saw the massive chocolate chip cookies and snagged two. As

Vince sat, Stone munched away too. "I gotta say one thing." Vince's mouth was half full of cookie. "Bailey and Albert are one dynamite duo."

Stone, his mouth too full to talk, just nodded.

Ice walked in toward the large screen, clicked on several buttons and picked up the remote. She stepped back and brought it online. The face of an older man appeared. "George, you're live. Go ahead," Ice said.

George's eyebrows lifted as he surveyed the table. "This darn technology." He shook his head. "I never would have figured this was possible. I'm sitting in my place, and you're sitting all the way over in Texas."

"For those of you who don't know, George is a scientist working in the Arctic."

Vince nodded. "Interesting place to be."

George nodded. "My life's work is here. If this global warming doesn't stop, we'll all be in trouble."

Vince didn't have anything to add to that because George was right. The world was in a crazy place right now. "I gather you have a problem there?"

"Not here," he said. "My daughter is currently working in the Galápagos Islands."

Vince sat up straighter, a grim look on his face. "Galápagos Islands? What is she doing there?"

"She's working on a government-funded study to assess the ecological damage of the tourist industry," he said heavily. "And I'm sure you can imagine her results will impact a lot of lives. It's a protected area, and only specific tours are allowed in and out. The local officials do what they can to control the damage, but there's been recent poaching."

"And what does poaching have to do with tourism?"

Stone asked.

Vince had to admit he didn't quite understand himself.

"We're not sure that one has anything to do with the other." Then George stopped, frowned and shook his head. "No, that's not quite true. We were considering they were connected. Until recently. Two tour guides had been left behind, to help with turtle counts. Both men turned up dead. It was thought they got in the poachers' way."

Slowly everybody in the room straightened. "Dead?" Ice asked. "How were they killed?"

"They were both shot in the head," George said. "I'm sure you can see why I'm a little concerned about my daughter."

"Have you spoken with her?" Levi asked.

"And have you talked to her about these concerns?" Vince was sure George had done that, but it still needed to be asked because why else was he calling Levi's team?

"I would if I could," he said. "I have spoken to her almost every day, but, for the last twenty-four hours, she's not answering her phone."

"Is she there with a team, or is she on her own?" Vince asked.

"A team," George said. "A very experienced team. So, as you can see I might be a little concerned."

"And because of the two tour guides being shot, you're assuming the worst, is that it?" Ice asked, her pencil moving rapidly on a scratch pad in front of her. "Do you have any visuals on her team? Anybody else answering their phones? Anybody else popping up at the local hotels? I presume she and her team are not staying on the island?"

"No, they stay on board the research ship. By a special dispensation, they were allowed to spend four days there while counting the turtle population. And that went off well. They've done this every year for several years to see the impact to the turtle numbers. This year was no different. It went off without a hitch. She was due to come back in another week. She did send me a weird email not too long ago." His voice was heavy. "In it she intimated this might be her last trip there. As she was struggling with some of the team members. Maybe it was nothing, I don't know. It just seemed an odd thing for her to say as she's not one to complain. She loves her work. She loves these animals. Normally she'd ignore everything else in order to help them."

"Meaning, one of her team might have been involved in poaching?" Vince frowned. "It would certainly be easy for the team to be involved in illegal operations when they're there and have such good connections."

"Exactly," George said. "But, like I said, the team is experienced, if not in the field then through their studies and their areas of expertise. She's worked with them many times. So I'm not sure if she's talking about poaching or something else."

"Sure, but maybe one person on that team is not quite as experienced," Levi said. "We've seen it time and time again, George. A team is only as good as its weakest link."

"I know," he said. "I've spoken to the local government. As far as they're concerned, there's absolutely nothing to worry about. I've spoken to other family members of the team, and again they all believe there's nothing to worry about. It's just something to do with me being me." He wrinkled up his face. "Yes, I'm a father, and all my instincts say something bad has happened."

"But there's been no contact, like from kidnappers? No

requests for ransom? No blackmail of any kind?" Vince asked. He hated to bring it up, but it was certainly one of the things first on his mind.

George shook his head violently. "No." Then he added slowly, "Not yet. There is still time, if they've been taken captive somewhere."

"And when you say *somewhere*," Stone said, "what do you mean?"

"I mean, taken to a second ship. So much of the work down there is done on ships. My daughter's team was on a big research vessel where they worked most of the time. It's quite possible somebody has taken over the research vessel or alternatively just took off some of the crew."

"To what purpose?"

"It's hard to say. The government contracts alone are worth millions," George said. "So who knows what kind of influence the team has, on both who gets the contracts and on whether the tourism dollars will get cut in order to allow the area to recover. There was open tourism until the government slapped those doors closed, and then installed just a few tours to bring some control back to the area. But, if that's not enough to bring the animal numbers back up and to stop further damage to the ecosystem, then the government will do more. Maybe the Galápagos Islands are closed for ten years. In a way, I'd like to see that. But it's very hard to determine what way they'll go. I don't have the data."

Ice, as if sensing he was heading off into research mode, brought the conversation back on topic.

George hesitated and then said, "I have to admit. I'm really worried about pirates."

There was silence in the kitchen.

Vince was the first to speak. "Okay, that's a word to make every father's heart crash."

"Exactly," George said heavily. "She's very much like me. We both went after our passions, and, because of that, we're often at opposite ends of the planet. I wasn't there a ton while she was growing up, but, since her mother died, we've become closer. I don't want to lose her. And if she's suffering at the hands of anybody ..." His face twisted up with anger. "Please make sure they pay for it."

Ice looked up from her notes. "I need her full name, contact information for the entire team, anybody you know in the government—ours and the local authorities—who have given the okay for her team to work there, and whoever you spoke with to date. The more names and contact info you can give us, the more chances we have of tracking down somebody who is there on the spot and who knows something."

"I'll email them to you." George smiled. "My daughter's name is Vanessa, and she has three more researchers with her, so four total on the team."

Stone chuckled. And then his face grew serious as George looked at him inquiringly. "The name," Stone said. "It's a great name for a woman."

George smiled wistfully. "It is, indeed. She was named after her grandmother. And that woman was a hell of a vixen," he said affectionately.

Ice turned to Vince, a smile on her face when she said, "Vince will head the mission to look into your daughter's disappearance. Send me that information, George, and we'll arrange flights to get him there as soon as we can."

"You're not sending him alone though, right?" George asked in alarm. "He'll need a team."

Ice smiled and nodded. "Not an issue. I've got one or two more guys we can send out."

"I can go," Stone said with a big grin. "I've never been there. I'd love to go." He looked up to see the screen was black. "I guess it's a good thing he was gone before I said that, huh?"

"You think?" Ice asked, raising her eyebrow. "But I get what you're saying. I haven't been either." She looked like she was figuring out the schedule, who she could juggle to add to this op. She looked at Vince. "You don't have any problem with that, do you?"

No," he said. "I don't. I can't say I've been to Galápagos either."

"You won't go alone," Levi said. "Give us a little bit, and we'll figure out who's going with you."

Ice looked at Levi. "Not many are here to choose from, and I think you said you always need to have, what? Four on hand here at all times?"

Levi nodded. "Yeah, that's what I said. We've got six now, but Merk is heading out tomorrow for California."

"Anybody new coming in?" Stone asked. "Didn't Ice say you had a transfer from Bullard's side coming?"

"Johan Wagner," Levi said slowly. "He is coming. I know the man from our visits over there. He was part of Bullard's security team for the new settlement on the Tunisia border. So he's got a lot of rough-and-ready and maybe even pirate experience." Levi stayed calm. "I should give him a go."

"We weren't expecting him until next week though," Ice interjected. "We'll have to see what his schedule looks like." She stood up. "I'll start on this. I'll let you know when and who and where." And she disappeared around the corner, the hard clip of her footsteps fading down the hall.

Stone looked at Vince. "This one is yours."

"Why is that?" Vince asked absentmindedly, his mind already considering the Galápagos Islands and pirates. He loved sailing. He loved the water. The Galápagos archipelago was on his list of places to see. He didn't really want to do a lame civilian tour though. And, as luck would have it— something very nice for a change—this job had just dropped in his lap.

"Starts with a *V*," Stone said with a smirk.

Vince stared at him in confusion. "What are you talking about?"

"The woman you'll rescue," he said. "Her name starts with a *V*."

Vince laughed. "So?"

"And named after her grandmother who was a *vixen*. So, she likely is too," Stone said with a head nod. "And that's a *V*. That makes her *Vince's Vixen*." He laughed. Standing up, he refilled his coffee, grabbed two more cookies and headed back to the security room. He was still laughing as he went down the hallway.

"Didn't you say something similar earlier?" Vince frowned at Levi who had half a smile playing at the corner of his mouth. "That really isn't working for me."

At that, Levi chuckled. "I did say that. But we'll see. That's not the issue. I suspect she won't be the only one who needs rescuing. If she's been separated from her team, maybe, but chances are the entire team has been taken out."

"Then the families should have heard something. No one else appears worried."

"George was always very intuitive of danger," Levi said. "I've known of several of his other research projects. One time, in the middle of the night, he hustled an entire town to move out, against the government and even the villagers' wishes. Later that entire side of the mountain came down in a mega-avalanche and buried eighty percent of the town."

Vince shook his head. "Wow. In other words, you trust that if he says something's wrong, it's worth checking out."

"Definitely. We can't afford to let time slip by. We already have five hours of traveling distance to get there if you could leave this instant. But the time zone change gains us one hour. So the net time change is four hours. Regardless, in those four-plus hours to get you to Houston's international airport and on a flight," he snapped, "all kinds of trouble could go down. We might get a trace on her for right now, but, by the time you land, it's a completely different story."

"Anybody close by you can haul in earlier?"

Levi tapped the tabletop as if running through his list of jobs and where all his men were.

Vince glanced around. "With your growing team here, you may have this covered electronically, but I almost feel like you need a wall map of the world and colored flag pins to assign to each man and to track who's in and who's out, and in what country, or at least what continent they're all in," he said with a laugh.

Levi nodded. "We're getting to that point, aren't we? We also have time off, holidays, marriages, all kinds of stuff going on," he said, in deep thought. "Have to make it work though."

"Are you okay with Johan?"

"I'd take Johan in a heartbeat," Levi said. "I'd also take his brother Jezeus. Both men are cut from the same cloth. They were raised in war times, turned into guerrilla fighters at the age of ten. Bullard pulled them out at fourteen, and it took until they were eighteen to stop the brainwashing, to straighten them up and to put them to work for him. Once they understood how allegiance actually worked, and the difference between the universally accepted concepts of right and wrong versus the skewed concepts of right and wrong of the man who had taken them prisoner, the brothers turned out to be incredible assets for Bullard."

"So why are they leaving him?"

Levi shook his head. "They're not leaving. We're doing a temporary switch, the brothers for Kasha and Brandon, who wanted to work over here for six months then for Bullard in Africa for six months—like those student exchange programs in high schools and colleges."

Vince nodded. "I might go for a deal like that too, down the road," he said with a smile. "It's a hell of a way to see the world."

"It's also a hell of a way to see that, no matter where you are in the world," Levi corrected as he stood, placing his cup on the table, heading for the door, "it's all the same."

SHE PULLED THE too-tight gag off her mouth, glad to breathe freely again. "Trussed up, tied up, whatever the hell you want to call it," Vanessa said as she lay on a hard bunk, "we're in a shit spot." The rest of her team were in various states of consciousness, tied up around her. All of them had been gagged too, with their hands tied behind them. Like her. To begin with at least.

Only not all of her team was here as she studied those around her. Dr. Laura Sanchez was missing. Vanessa's heart filled with dread. Vanessa had been alone in the lab when attacked by two gunmen. In the process she'd been knocked unconscious, only to wake up with her team around her—minus Laura.

These gunmen were serious, and they had nothing to do with the research her team was here to conduct. These men were either pirates or poachers. And that just broke her heart. Poachers were the bane of any research group looking to preserve the life of a species.

Species at risk was one of the areas that made Vanessa's heart bleed. And to see poachers stealing eggs, shooting and killing the turtles, broke her heart and made her realize once again that the most dangerous predators in the world were its humans. Half the time they killed not for food or out of necessity but for sheer pleasure. And humans were one of the few species to kill each other as wantonly as they did everything else.

She tried once again to wriggle her hands free. They were in front of her now, only because she'd managed to slip them down over her butt and up in front of her legs. She was average height for a woman with fairly short legs, and that made the job a little easier. Across from her, Dr. Willard Walker watched her, hope in his eyes. She tried hard to bite the knots free, but the rope was nylon, and her teeth weren't cutting through. She collapsed back down, breathing heavily.

They could hear footsteps above them. The boat itself was fairly rickety. She imagined whoever had kidnapped them had taken over their research vessel as spoils of war. And, if that was the case, what boat was she on now? The research vessel was a wonderful ship, and she'd do a lot to reclaim it. The last thing she wanted was to be treated as somebody who didn't matter. Somebody who was just a means to an end.

She'd spent her lifetime looking for attention from her

parents, who were both scientists, so involved in their own work sometimes that she had to be an outright nasty child in order to get them to look up at her. They'd been confused and surprised and never really understood her. Never understood what drove her. But then she hadn't really understood what had driven them either, until she became a teenager and got hooked on saving as many animals as she could. Then she understood completely.

For that reason alone, she decided there was no way in hell she would have a family. She wouldn't do to her children what her parents had done to her. She'd grown past that sense of insecurity and neediness but still had no plans to repeat the cycle.

A muffled sound came across from her. Her eyes flew open to see Dr. Walker motioning toward her bound hands again. She stared down at them as she lifted them up. They were already torn and bleeding, but she knew she had to get them loose. She studied the hard edge of the board where she lay, wondering if any frayed edges could saw away on her ropes.

She sat up, swung her legs over the edge and worked the ropes up and down the sides of the wood. She knew at some point it would work, but she didn't know if she had enough hours or energy. She'd lost track of time. Surely they'd been kidnapped at least twenty-four hours ago, with very little food and water, only what they had on them. If she didn't know better, she'd think the damn kidnappers planned on letting them slowly die down here.

She knew she and her crew were worth money. But, in order to exchange her team for said money, she'd have to let their kidnappers know her team had value. And that was a catch-22. Because, to gain the kidnappers' attention, they took a chance on getting another beating.

She wasn't sure what the kidnappers were smuggling. Because of the location, she wondered if it was turtles. But it could also be that the gunmen were just using a sacred spot to hold and move goods that had nothing to do with the actual habitat. Since the archipelago was shut down for tours right now, it made for very little traffic back and forth. As she thought about it, that was a smart move on the kidnappers' part.

Tony made a strangled sound in the back of his throat.

She turned and looked at their valuable research assistant. This was his first on-site job, and he'd been thrilled to join them. That it had turned into his biggest nightmare was something she had no control over.

He lifted and humped his butt several times.

She studied his face, and he kept motioning with his head to his side. She hopped off the bunk, hobbled over with great difficulty, her ankles still bound, using the bunk to walk. When she got to him on the floor, she crouched beside him to see a shape in his pocket, then dove her fingers in and pulled out a penknife. She snapped it open, cut her own ties and then cut him loose and went around systematically cutting everyone else free.

Finally with everybody untied, they stared at each other. She handed the pocketknife back to Tony. "I'm so glad you thought to bring that," she whispered. "Anyone see Dr. Laura?"

They all shook their heads.

Tony asked, "How do we get out of here?"

She bolted to look out the small porthole window. "There's only water on this side," she said.

Tony checked the other side and nodded. "Here too."

"So, on three sides, we're looking at endless ocean," Dr. Walker said. "That leaves only one other direction. We don't have any tools. We have no weapons except for a small pocketknife."

She turned and smiled, baring her teeth, holding up the ropes she'd cut off. "And these."

Tony nodded. "And rope. You're right. If we can get behind the kidnappers, we could strangle them."

"There's four of us and at least two gunmen that I know of," she snapped, her voice low and hard. "If need be, I'll be the tease, bring them into the room. You guys will have to go after them."

The men nodded.

Dr. Walker asked, "Do you really think their end game is our deaths?"

"How much water have you had in the last twenty-four hours?" Tony asked.

For that, Dr. Walker had no reply.

She checked her pockets. "Everybody see what you have. Phones, lighters, anything."

"What would you do with a lighter?" Dr. Walker asked curiously.

"Torch the boat," she said.

Just as she said it, they heard footsteps overhead once again. They stopped talking to listen, their ears strained to hear if anybody would come down below. So far they'd had one visitor the whole time, that they knew of, and that was to put a bucket of water down. And that was it. It was pretty damn hard to drink when your mouths were gagged, and you were tied up.

Vanessa dropped down, picked up the bucket and very gently sipped from it. She wrinkled her nose. "It's not the best, but it'll do." She handed it around to the others until everybody had had a drink.

"You wouldn't burn the boat, would you?" Dr. Walker asked.

She shot him a hard look. "If it's our only way to get out of here? Yes."

"That'll throw us into the ocean," he said, "where we could be ten times worse off."

She smiled at him. That was the difference between her and Dr. Walker. He was all about the research, all about his glass of port in the evening and his lattes in the morning. Whereas she was all about Mother Nature. And, if there was one thing she understood, Mother Nature was a bitch. And she was very unkind to some animals. When your time was up, your time was up. But Mother Nature also allowed each and every animal to fight to the end. And, if that was the case right now, Vanessa had absolutely no trouble taking these assholes down with her.

"If it'll be us or them, and we'll die anyway," she added quietly, "I'll make sure I take them with me."

Tony nodded. "I hope it doesn't come to that—not to mention that Dr. Laura could be up there, captive as well—but I agree."

They looked over at Jasper, another research student who was working on his PhD thesis. He was still out cold, but then he'd taken a heavy blow to the head, whereas the others had been not quite so bashed. Something about Jasper's size always seemed to get him into trouble. Everybody wanted to challenge him, to see if they could beat him. That was hardly fair, but it didn't really matter. Some things were a cross to bear. Jasper was at least six feet, five inches tall and weighed 280 pounds. But he was all teddy bear.

18

Now if they could only get him to wake up.

She crouched beside him and smacked his cheek lightly. "Jasper, come on, wake up."

He moaned gently.

She bent down, placed her mouth against his ear and said, "Don't talk. Don't make a sound. We've been kidnapped by a pirate ship or a bunch of poachers. We're being held in the hull of their boat. But we have now cut all our ties, and we're loose. You're the only one not conscious."

His eyes fluttered open, and he stared at her in confusion.

She smiled down at him. "You're mostly all right. You got hit on the head though. Sit up slowly, and see if you can move around."

He blinked several times. It took another moment for him to focus and then to react. He sat up slowly, wincing as the blood flowed again through his body with his movements. With her help and the bunk beside him, he stretched to his full height. He let his breath rush out and half closed his eyes. "It's not too bad," he muttered. "I've always had a hard head. I don't know what they hit me with, but it hurts like hell."

"Likely they hit you with the butt of a rifle because you wouldn't go down. You always were someone who didn't know when to quit," Dr. Walker said.

Jasper's lopsided grin slipped out. "Yeah, that's not my style." He looked around, and his gaze narrowed. "Man, my head hurts." He rotated his head gently on his neck and groaned slightly.

"As long as you live through this, you're good," Vanessa said, "but there's no sign of Laura. She's not here with us. That's all we know."

He stared at her in shock.

She reached an arm around Jasper and hugged him close. He was only twenty-two, one of those real brainiac overgrown boys. But he was steady. And that, she needed. She glanced at the other two. "We need a plan," she said.

"One that doesn't involve burning the boat," Dr. Walker said drily.

Just then they heard footsteps coming down the stairs and panicked. Dr. Walker and Tony collapsed onto their bunks where she had cut their bonds, drew up, as if tied still, and pretended to be unconscious. She couldn't do anything about their gags. She motioned at Jasper to do the same. He lay on the floor again and tucked his feet under a bunk to hide that his feet were no longer bound. And he lay with his hands behind his back as if still unconscious.

She was the one who would have a harder time hiding her lack of ropes on her wrists and ankles. And, if she couldn't surprise her kidnappers, then there wasn't a whole lot she could do otherwise. She scrunched down to the lower end of the bunk, dropped her feet off the back side and crumpled sideways. All she needed was a chance for somebody to get in far enough for her to attack. Because, once she did that, no way in hell would she let them take her down. She wasn't vicious by nature, but she sure as hell wasn't someone who would give up, lie down and let them kill her just because they wanted to.

The door opened, and an unarmed man walked in.

Her eyes slitted open, looking under her eyelashes, she watched him as he stepped inside, looked at the still-full bucket and snorted. "How long are you guys planning on sleeping?" he asked with a snort. He picked up the bucket and tossed water into Jasper's face on the floor.

Instantly she exploded off her bunk and, with a rope in

her hands, wrapped it tight around his neck and pulled it and twisted it hard. He hardly made a sound as he struggled forward, but Dr. Walker pulled his knees out from under him, and he went down—yanking Vanessa to the floor with him. She let go of the rope before it further tore up her hands and rolled away. Meanwhile, Jasper grabbed the bucket and slammed him hard over the head. And, just like that, they had one man down.

Slowly she pulled herself toward him and checked his pulse.

"Did you kill him?" Tony asked, his voice harsh, yet hopeful.

She shook her head. "No. More's the pity. Because we should. You know that, right?"

She hated hearing those words coming from her mouth, but the only way they would get out of this alive was if they picked off each and every one of their captors to make sure they couldn't get back up again.

Jasper had a different answer. He picked up the bucket again and hit the man over the head once more. Jasper then grabbed the ropes, tied up the man's hands behind him, and his legs, then joined his bindings with another rope and pulled his legs tight up against his back. He stuffed a gag into the man's mouth so he couldn't make a sound. And then, with help, the man was shoved under a bunk. These were attached to the wall with hinges, allowing them to be lifted and lowered.

She stared at their captive and realized it was the best they could do. He would survive, or he wouldn't. But then that was the same story for themselves. With the door open, Vanessa slipped to the edge and peered around the corner. Another room was up front and a kitchen. Then the deck above. She had no clue how many men were here.

As she looked back, she saw Jasper going through the man's pockets. She smiled. Too bad he hadn't come down with a gun. Jasper pulled out money and his ID, shrugged, put everything into his own pocket and dropped the bunk down over the man. Then he picked up the bucket and one of the other ropes and motioned at her.

She nodded, looked at the other two, who stood in line behind Jasper. Then again, that was probably the best place to be. He was an indomitable force that would be hard to get through. She slipped forward, keeping her back against the wall as she checked out the first room, which was a storeroom and empty of humans. But there was food, and that was good. Who knew what they might need as they moved on? Knowing she didn't have the time, but still looking for weapons, she stepped inside to search for something.

She came up with an old cast-iron frying pan on the bottom shelf. She handed it to Dr. Walker. He frowned, then hefted it and smiled at her. She went back in the storage room to search for more. But there just didn't appear to be anything else suitable for defending themselves. She came back out, shrugged at Tony and kept going. She stopped just ahead of the kitchen area, peered around the corner and smiled. It was empty.

She slid inside around the table area and over to the kitchen. There she grabbed three big knives and came back. She traded Jasper's bucket for a big butcher knife. She gave a filet knife to Tony, and for herself she had a chef's knife. In her other hand, she carried a cleaver. She smiled. "I don't know how many men are up above, but we need to find out. The sooner we're back in control, the sooner we're out of this nightmare."

Just as she said that, she heard footsteps on the stairs.

Chapter 2

A *CLICK* OF a gun alerted her first.

Swearing softly under his breath, the man coming down the stairs froze. She could see the rifle barrel, just the tip of it, pointing downward. And then he slowly backed up. And, just like that, the double doors to the hatch above closed down on top of them.

She swore under her breath. "What the hell gave us away?"

"Instinct. The fact that his buddy didn't respond or return again likely," Dr. Walker said. He looked around. "So we've got a kitchen, and we've got weapons, but he's got all the rifles. Still you don't bring a knife to a gun fight," he snapped. "As long as we're here, stuck, with them above us, you know we aren't getting anywhere."

Jasper climbed the stairs and put his shoulder and his back to the hatch. They could see it lift slightly but also saw the big lock on top, with huge wrought iron hinges, which had them locked in, and Jasper couldn't lift it any higher. Grim-faced, they turned to look at each other.

"Next idea?" the men asked her.

But she was out of ideas. She took a look out the window and said, "There's land behind us."

They gathered around to see because, if they could reach land anywhere, they'd take that chance. Swimming would be a bitch if it was too far, and, if the weather turned on them, they could forget it. They were already up against some of the world's worst predators in the water.

"We won't make it," Dr. Walker said calmly. He looked up at the sky. "A storm's coming."

And, sure enough, even as he said it, they could see the clouds rolling toward them.

"So this is checkmate," he said in a dour tone. "Unless you have any final moves, this is as far as we go."

She stared at him. "I'm not giving up yet."

Dr. Walker nodded. "Maybe not, but I've got a splitting headache, so I'm lying down. When you guys figure out what plan B is of this insane suicide mission, you can wake me." He walked back to the small cabin area and collapsed on one of the bunks.

She turned to look at Tony and Jasper. "Any suggestions?"

One by one they looked at her and shook their heads.

"Nothing," Jasper said. "We have to get upstairs. There's not really any way to do that."

Defeated and furious, she sagged into one of the chairs at the kitchen table. "There's got to be a way."

"Maybe," Jasper said. "But we haven't found it yet."

VINCE WAS ALREADY on his phone. He stood at the dock, staring out to where the last boat-for-hire had just left. Supposedly there wasn't another one he could rent for miles. He didn't believe one word the locals were telling him. Somebody had paid a ton of money to keep them all quiet, and he didn't appreciate that.

He was on hold, awaiting a talk with another one of the

local government officials. Vince wanted one of their boats, and they weren't having anything of it. They couldn't be involved, according to them. Whatever happened had to be done quietly. There were enough factions here to contend with that, if it looked like the US government was helping one, the authorities here would get shit from the others.

"And what about the pirates who potentially have taken a US research ship?"

"But you can't prove that, can you?" said the next man in line at the other end in that officious voice. "We've lost contact. A storm is brewing. For all you know, the team has just been caught up in the storm. Maybe their batteries ran out. Maybe one of them has been injured, and the others are hiking, out looking for help. There are all kinds of scenarios and not enough time for anything to have been determined."

"Which is why I'm trying to find them," he snapped.

"And we wish you well," the man said. *Click*.

Vince stared at his phone. "That officer's an idiot," he said. "Just a little desk operator who doesn't want to get his hands dirty, wants it all to go away so he can check a little box on his paperwork to say done, as long as it didn't have anything to do with him."

"That's what desk jockeys are," Johan said. But his voice was lighthearted, almost laughing.

Vince turned and frowned at him. "Did you find a boat?"

"Not only did I find a boat," he said, "but I found a nice sailboat."

"Where is it?" Vince turned to study the marina.

"It's coming," Johan said. "Bullard had a friend—Lexi— who was already down here. He's quite happy to lend it our way. Apparently pirates gave Lexi a run for his money on a different trip, and, if there's anything we can do to take out one group, he's more than willing to help us. And, if it costs him his boat, it's insured."

Vince's eyebrows rose. "Seriously?" At Johan's chuckle and nod, Vince just shook his head. "Some people have more money than God."

"Yeah, that's Lexi," Johan said. "He made it in the dot-com era before the crash, and, since then, he's on easy street, living off his investments."

"That's the life," Vince said. On the other hand he didn't think he could do it himself. A life without purpose for him would be one long endless boring day.

"He's pretty damn happy about it," Johan said. "We're a little short on supplies though."

"It's almost like the pirates pay better than we do," Vince complained good-naturedly.

"They do. It's the only way to buy silence around here. It's either pay better or the punishment is worse." He pointed at several boxes he had stacked beside him. "I figure we got enough for a couple days. If we're picking up the science team, we could run into trouble. So, if we can get a line on more foodstuffs, it would help." His phone rang just then.

Vince waited as Johan spoke to whoever was on the other end.

When he hung up, he said, "Lexi's boat left the marina. It'll be here in about thirty minutes."

"And what about the other issue?" Vince asked. "Did Bullard have any luck with that?"

"No, but Levi came through. In places like this, you can buy anything," he said, "and guns are no different. We have a delivery coming soon."

"We're trusting an awful lot of local people," Vince said cautiously.

"Look," Johan said. "I know you are lead on this op. But have you ever been here before?"

"Nope," Vince said with a headshake.

"So I hope you don't mind if I take the lead on some things, since I know the area and have some local contacts. Just tell me if you think I'm out of line."

"Agreed," Vince said, and the guys shook hands.

As much as he liked this guy Johan, Vince didn't know him from Adam. But, so far, it was just the two of them. Then again, Vince had said he would go, even if just the two of them, because a small stealthy team was better in some cases. Two men didn't make as much of a ripple as four. And, when going after something like this, the smaller the better.

Levi had reluctantly agreed, but only because he was sending two more as soon as he could get it to happen. They were coming, would sit in waiting, ready to help Vince and Johan in any way as they tied this up. On that note, Vince and Johan had each taken off as fast as they could with multiple hops—Vince from Houston and Johan from who-knows-where—and, when they'd arrived in Galápagos, they'd met up and had pulled together their supplies.

That was when they ran into trouble. First off, they couldn't find a boat to rent. Then they couldn't get supplies. But it seemed like they just needed to sweeten the pot with a little more money to grease the local wheels. Particularly as Vince and Johan needed weapons—and not just one or two. That was nonnegotiable.

"So our gun shipment is being delivered here?" Vince searched the docks. This was not a delivery he wanted in a public location or done in broad daylight.

Johan nodded. "I think it's coming in the boat."

Vince's expression cleared. "That makes sense." He waved his arm to the busy market just behind them past the marina's docks. "I wasn't sure how we were supposed to get deliveries through that place."

Johan chuckled. "Well, there're ways, but this is a subtler one."

"Good," Vince said. "I'm not getting anywhere with the bloody government officials."

"Screw them," Johan said. "We don't need anything from them. Ice has contacted the rest of the families of the missing team. She just sent me a text to say nobody has heard from any of them. And while that worried them, they were all pleased to note that no demands for ransom had come through either."

"So we're looking for four missing persons for sure – possibly five as there seems to be some uncertainty here?"

Johan nodded. "So far, that's the intel we are working on. George must be beside himself."

"He is, but he also trusts Levi. So the sooner we can get this done, the better." They still had a few things to check off. Vince said, "I'll head to the market and see if I can get a bit more fresh food to take with us. We could be out there for a week, searching the Pacific Ocean for one lost ship."

"Be back in twenty," Johan said. "When the boat arrives, we won't have a minute to spare."

Vince took off running. He'd seen a fresh food and veggie market not far away. He wanted to make sure he and Johan at least had food supplies to last the two of them one week but also to feed the team members. Yet what he really wanted was to make sure they had *medical* supplies. As he wandered the market with an eye on the time, he picked up several items.

Then he stopped at what appeared to be a drugstore on the street. As he sought bandages, he quickly put together a first aid kit and packed it up.

When he walked back down the dock, right on time, he saw a beautiful white almost research-looking sailboat come into the marina. He stepped up beside Johan and asked, "Is this it?"

"It's old, as in very old. The original owner was a scientist, but Lexi bought it off him. Lexi's got a yacht too of course, for fun. He brought both boats down here with him, thinking he could rent one or just swap about between the two, should one need repairs or whatever. But he said this is the one you want when you're heading into ugly weather. It's also the one more likely to get past the pirates, so you can get to where you want to go," he said. "I wouldn't say no. We needed anything Lexi could give us."

With that, the men boarded. Command changed hands as the captain and his first mate stepped off, and, without further ado, Vince and Johan pushed away from the dock and headed out.

"Did we check for fuel?" Vince asked.

"The captain fully loaded it, per Lexi's instructions," Johan said. "We're good to go."

Moving the supplies downstairs, Vince stopped in surprise. It looked like the owner had prestocked the boat. There were boxes of dry goods, huge restaurant-size canned goods sitting on the floor, some fresh food as well. They had enough food here for a month, from the looks of it. Vince chuckled when he saw the toilet paper. Something he hadn't even thought of. He shook his head.

"Glad somebody was thinking." He turned and headed toward the kitchen, opening the cupboards and putting things away.

When he got underneath the veggies, he saw two large crates. He knew what those were. He bent, popped one open and whistled. In front of him were four gleaming assault rifles, with clips, and one even had a belt. He picked them up, hefted them and stared in amazement. They were brand new. Where the hell had Lexi gotten these? In the second box were several handguns. And look at that—grenades!

Stowing everything nicely under the table, he crawled up to the top deck and said to Johan, "I don't know what *friend* this is of Bullard's, but, when he loaded us for bear, he loaded us for grizzly bear."

Johan laughed. "That's exactly what we need. It might not be bears we're hunting, but it'll be assholes nonetheless."

Chapter 3

VANESSA AND HER team hadn't heard anything since the hatch had been dropped and locked. No footsteps, no voices, nothing. Their captive also hadn't moved. She didn't know if Jasper's blows to the head had done in the man or if she'd actually strangled him enough to have done some serious damage.

It was hard to feel sorry for him. This was how the kidnappers had treated her and her team. What did he expect? This was already a shit deal, and the last thing she wanted was any more of it. But she'd been checking the ceilings to see if there was any hatch or something loose, any way they could pry some of the ceiling boards out. The men had just watched her as she'd gone from board to board, testing each for a weakness.

When she'd asked Jasper to help, the two had repeated her efforts, yet found nothing. She had the porthole windows she knew she could get out of—if they even opened. She was the only one small enough to make it through. But she wasn't sure she could swing around and get up on the deck. And, if they couldn't open the portholes, once they punched a hole in the glass, it would alert whoever was above that their captives were coming. Not only that, if they ran into ugly weather, that broken window itself could end up causing their death, flooding them inside, if not capsizing the boat too. It wouldn't be fun to sink in the sea.

The waves continued to slap against the side of the boat, although they seemed to be stronger and to happen more often. The only saving grace right now was they had access to the kitchen, and that meant some food. The men had opened cans of beans and what looked like peaches. They found a loaf of bread and what appeared to be rice. They'd eaten as much as they wanted, their stomachs still woozy and uncertain, but it had worked for the moment.

What she really needed was to find a way to open that damn hatch. Plus, Vanessa was worried about Laura. If she was up on deck, separated from the others, why? And what did these men want? What had happened to their research vessel? It was worth a lot of money. The university leased it out to other companies and universities for research trips. It would be insured, but still. All their research data was on board too.

She studied the wood of the hatch. If there was even an ax, she could chop it open. She didn't give a shit if the kidnappers knew she was coming or not. Even if they heard her, and even if they fired into the hatch and shot her, no way the gunmen upstairs would come farther into the hull, the team could hide in enough places that the kidnappers wouldn't know for sure where the three men were. The best thing for their captors would be to abandon ship and to sink it.

She winced at the thought. She surprised herself at the nasty turn of her mind if she was thinking *that* was the best avenue. But it was what she'd do if a ship was full of assholes, and she had no other way to lose them. She would sink the damn boat and all of them with it.

The boat listed to one side and then turned around. The

men looked at her. She nodded grimly. "I know. I don't think anybody's piloting this thing. Or if it's been abandoned."

At the word *abandoned*, their eyes lit with hope, and then they frowned.

"Would they do that?" Dr. Walker asked.

"It depends how many are involved," she said. "Think about it. If the kidnappers have a second boat, they could be on that boat and just watching us."

"But we didn't see one."

"But we can't see behind us," she said. "So I'm not saying that's what they're doing, but it's certainly possible."

They nodded, but nobody was happy with her words.

"What's the chance they'll just sink us then?" Tony asked nervously.

"That's what I would do," she said honestly. "Think about it. If they can't get in here without endangering themselves, then they have to get rid of us one way or another. Or they just leave us here to float. It's not like we're going anywhere. They can come back and collect us later."

"You really do have a nasty mind-set, don't you?" Dr. Walker said.

She chuckled. "It's not the easiest place to be right now, but we're free. We have food. We're walking around. We're dry for the moment. And, for all we know, we're in a decent seaworthy vessel."

"Well, we could be in something that's ready to sink," Dr. Walker said. "And then what?"

"Then what?" she said sadly. "What is it you want me to say? I have no better idea how to get up there than you do. We'll have to ride out this storm and see."

"None of us have our phones either," Tony said.

"The kidnappers can't get any reception out here in the storm," Jasper said. "The best we can do is get into the engine room and see if we can send a message from there."

She nodded. "In that case, it's back to finding a way to open that damn hatch."

"You'll open the hatch and take a bullet?" Dr. Walker asked, bewildered. "Don't you give a damn?"

"Not particularly," she said, "because, if we sit here, we could take a bullet too. Either that or we could drown. Whether by the sea or by the gunmen, it's drowning all the same."

"Do you have any new ideas?" Jasper asked, dismissing the locked hatch above and instead staring at the wooden ceiling. "We could probably use the assorted kitchen knives to cut out a new hatch, but that'll take forever."

"That'll only work," she said, "if there is no second flooring above."

"Which there will be," Dr. Walker said. "Why don't you rest a minute? There's really nothing we can do."

"So we're supposed to just stay here adrift and wait until somebody decides to pick us up or to pick us off?" she asked in exasperation. "You *do* know that you have to help yourself and that you can't just wait and hope that someone comes along in this vast ocean and rescues us, right?"

Her tone had him backing up a step.

"Sometimes *you* have to rescue *yourself*." She turned her back on Dr. Walker and studied the hatch again. Her fighting spirit was truly aroused at this point. "There has to be some way to unscrew or demobilize the hinges."

"If you mean, trying to open it, I've searched for a screwdriver," Jasper said, studying the stairs. "But I haven't found anything. These are really heavy duty welds in here."

She groaned. "Of course. It's a great seaworthy old boat. Probably been in service for decades. I hate to ruin her myself, but I don't plan on letting that storm drown us. Or having some assholes open the door suddenly and come in with machine guns and take us out."

"We don't have a whole lot of other choices," Jasper said. "Again there's a limit to what we can do."

Frustrated and angry, she threw herself onto the chair and stretched out. "In that case, I'll have a nap," she said angrily. And of course, what that really meant was, *Don't talk to me unless you have some plan to get us out of here.*

VINCE AND JOHAN could see the storm brewing up ahead. Johan studied it and smiled. "That one'll be a doozy."

"Yeah," Vince said, standing at his side. "I don't have much in the way of coordinates for the last time the research crew was seen. But we have their ship—which nobody has seen or reported to have heard from in almost two days now—about fourteen nautical miles off the Galápagos Islands. They were apparently moored out to sea where they were doing their research work. Far enough away for any storm to batter them, but apparently it was a prime distance for the type of work they were doing."

"Whatever the hell that means," Johan said with a smirk. "Probably was just a nice spot."

"Agreed," Vince said with a laugh. "But that gives us a general direction. Unless the pirates have taken them and moved them away. Or moved them off their research boat onto another one, but I don't know why they would do that."

"Because the research vessel is probably worth a lot of

money," Johan said. "If you think about it, there's a lot of money in the electronics alone."

"True enough," Vince said, tapping the paper map in front of him. "From the looks of it, we're almost a full day out."

"We're going at a pretty good clip," he said, "but we're burning through a lot of gas. I'm hoping, when we get there, somebody has spare fuel for us."

"But we have two tanks with us, correct?" Vince turned to look back on the decks. Two big tanks of fuel sat on the flat main deck area, one on either side of the sailboat, plus two rowboats, one on either side. Down below was one lab, which was old and no longer in use, and the kitchen and bunks for the staff and crew.

"Yes. We should check to make sure both really are full."

"I'll do that," Vince said.

He made his way down the four steps to the main deck and checked on the fuel tanks. There was a small ladder on the side. He climbed up, opened the tank nozzle at the top and tried to peer in. When that didn't work, he pulled up his flashlight on his phone and used that to help him see the reflection inside. Sure enough, it was almost full. Buoyed by that thought, he closed the opening and made his way to the second one. It was full too. Satisfied, he made his way in the high winds back up to the pilot station. "Yes, both are full," he said.

"Okay. We'll take shifts. So, if I'm driving now, you've got meal prep duty. Then we'll switch out and start four-hour sleeping rounds."

"Good enough," Vince said and headed to the kitchen, looking to see what they had that he could pull together. There was a lot of fresh food but not much meat. He managed to make a thick stew within forty minutes.

As he cleaned up, waiting for the meal to finish cooking, he thought he heard the engine churning in a different tone. Frowning, turning off the heat under the food, making sure the pot was secure in case the weather picked up, he made his way back upstairs. There he crawled up the stairs to the pilot station and asked, "What's that I'm hearing?"

"I had to tone her down," Johan said, pointing at the storm coming toward them. "That's looking pretty nasty. I'm trying to avoid it as much as I can. But we need to hit as close to a straight line to our target as we can make it."

"Correct," Vince said, studying the storm. "We hardly have gear for that kind of weather."

"Doesn't matter," Johan said. "This boat has handled that and much worse. We need to make sure we're able-bodied when we arrive because there's just two of us, and there's no way to know how many pirates or poachers that we'll be up against." He glanced at Vince. "Did you get any food together?"

Vince nodded. "I've got a hot stew down there."

"Good enough," Johan said. "I'll set this on autopilot. Let's go eat."

The two men made their way down below. Vince realized he had barely enough clothing for this adventure. When he got a minute, he'd check the cupboards in the bunk room, see if there was any spare gear. If that storm hit, even though they were in warm equator climates, it would be cold, and hypothermia would set in fast.

They both downed two big bowls of stew with some big chunks of bread. After he cleaned up, Vince asked, "Are you okay to keep piloting the boat? Or you want me to relieve you now?"

Johan looked at his watch. "We'll switch at midnight." And he headed up again.

Left to his own devices, Vince packed away the leftovers, checked in the bunk room, found a couple heavy coats, which made him smile. These were perfect, given the ugly weather approaching. He brought them out and hung them up where they would be easily available as he kept digging. He also found several pairs of gloves and boots. All good stuff.

Then he turned his attention to the weapons. If they weren't fully loaded, they were useless when needed. He set them out and carefully checked them over, making sure everything was clean and operational. Afterward he loaded them and set them to one side and then worked on the handguns.

By the time midnight came, the lights flickered beside him. He felt the fatigue. Not that there was any help for it. His shift was next up. Leaving the weapons in order as he'd laid them out, he made his way topside with a hot mug of coffee, leaving the rest of the pot down below for Johan to consume.

Up above Johan was smiling as the waves built. "You're in for a bitch of a ride," he said. "If it gets too rough, I'll come up. It's easier to ride out when you're on top."

"You need sleep," Vince said.

"Yeah? And how much did you get?"

Vince shook his head. "I didn't. But the weapons are ready to go."

Johan slapped him on the shoulder. "Now that's what I like. Food and weapons. The only two things a man needs."

Vince could think of something else that he'd like, but he wouldn't bring it up now.

As soon as Johan made his way down below, Vince took over the wheel, feeling something inside him settle as he slowly got his sea legs in the small pilot room. Nothing but darkness was out there, except for the lights on the boat itself. The waves were battering them around pretty good. They were consuming a lot of fuel, still racing forward and fighting this storm as he headed down the path Johan had laid.

They were skirting the outside of the storm as much as possible, hoping to pick up speed by avoiding the bulk of the resistance. He smiled at the moon above. There was a lot to be said for being out on an ocean like this. He would prefer a better reason for it, but this night was still special. There was something magical about being in a boat in the middle of the ocean in the middle of the night, just feeling the waves crashing against the pieces of wood that held you back from the frigid cold waters of the deep ocean. The elements of Mother Nature were something to behold. And he knew he wouldn't forget this night for a long time to come.

He just hoped Vanessa was in a position to find something good in this night too.

Chapter 4

V ANESSA'S HEAD ROSE at an odd sound. "Do you guys
hear that?"

But the men were sound asleep.

She got up slowly and looked out the window. Nothing
was there but calmer seas and a mild gray sky. It looked like
the storm had passed. She patted the wall of the old vessel
beside her affectionately. "I knew you could do it, girl.
You've already seen many storms like that one, haven't you?"

It had helped that they were on the outskirts of the
storm, and so the boat hadn't been in a direct line of its fury.
She wasn't sure that this old vessel would have handled that.
It seemed like the boat had just spun endlessly, tossed in the
water like a toy. Because of that, she was afraid no pilot at all
was on board. And that just made her angry.

She checked the other windows but couldn't see anything. With the men still sleeping, she walked back up the
stairs and once again tested the hatch doors. Of course, they
were still locked. She had to admit by now that her biggest
nightmare was her fear that she would be left floating in the
ocean until somebody found their corpses.

She and her team had already discussed the rationing of
their stores of food—that they weren't sharing with anybody
above deck apparently—but that didn't mean there was
enough for them down here for long. Fresh water would

become an issue soon too. She was still interested in opening one of the portholes somehow, even if breaking them. She'd do what she could to get out of here. If the portholes opened, all the better, but they didn't look like it. The metal looked rusted shut.

She went back to the hatch and sat on the stairs. Only to straighten, straining to sort out the noises she heard again. Or thought she heard. Was that another boat arriving? She was sure another engine chugged alongside them. She raced from porthole to porthole, looking to see what vessel it was. Was it their captors returning? Or rescuers? At the last porthole, she saw a small research vessel coming toward them. She cried out in joy and woke the three men.

It took the men a few minutes to shake the sleep from their eyes and to understand. Then they were up, staring out of the windows with her.

When the boat came up alongside and threw a line to their boat, she was surprised when two men nimbly hopped across and tied the two boats so they bumped along together. She could hear somebody outside calling out if anybody was on board.

She pounded on the hatch; then Jasper pulled her back. "Hey, remember? We don't know who these men are."

"Maybe," she said, "but they're our only chance of getting out of here."

He nodded and grabbed the frying pan they had planned to use as a weapon and banged it against the hatch door.

A voice called out, "We're coming. Hang on."

And suddenly the hinges were popped, and the latch was flung open wide. She made her way up the stairs, with the others coming along behind her.

She spun to look at their rescuers. "Is anybody else on

board?"

The two men shook their heads. "It looks like it's just you guys."

She grinned, threw her arms around the man closest to her and hugged him tight. "Thank you, thank you, thank you. We were kidnapped and moved into the bottom of this boat, and they locked the hatch on us. One of the captors is down below. We heard him before he came in one time. I guess the other took off. Although I have no idea where he went." Confused, she walked to the front of the boat. "This is a really old boat. No wonder the portholes didn't open." She turned to look at the two strangers. "Did you come to rescue us?"

The men looked at her. The one she'd hugged asked, "Are you Vanessa Blanchard?"

Surprised, she nodded. "You did come to rescue us, didn't you?"

He grinned. "Yeah. So far it's been easier and faster than we expected. We just went to your ship's last recorded location, and here you are."

She smiled. "So you found our research ship?"

Vince shook his head. "Not yet. But we're hoping it's nearby."

"And you'll search for it?" she asked, looking from man to man.

"We will."

"So, who sent you? Who knew we were in trouble? We didn't even get a chance to send out SOS signals."

"Your father," Vince said, looking at everyone's body language.

Her face lit up. "Well, doesn't that figure. We spoke almost every day. I guess, when I missed a day's call, he decided I was in trouble." She grinned at the others. "This is a great day after all." She looked at the small research vessel that had pulled up beside them. "So who are you guys besides the men my father sent?"

"We work for Legendary Security," said the man she'd hugged. He held out his hand. "I'm Vince Manoj, and this is Johan Wagner."

Everyone shook hands.

"We'd better get the man up from down below," Johan said.

She led the way back down and pointed him out. "And we're missing one of our team."

Vince shot her a look, then said, "Let's get the injured man first."

The two men pulled him out from under the bunk, checking him over. They looked at her. "That head injury is bad. Not sure he'll make it."

She nodded grimly. "I wasn't sure me and my team would make it either, but this really was life and death."

The two men grabbed the kidnapper's legs and shoulders and carefully carried him up to the deck. "He needs medical attention."

She stared down at her captor. "He's so young, isn't he? I couldn't see that down there." She felt terrible.

"No reason for you to consider his age," Vince said. "When you're under attack like that, all you can do is defend yourselves and try to escape."

"He wasn't alone, so where is the other kidnapper? And where is Laura? We're missing our fifth team member," Vanessa said, looking up at him. "Dr. Laura Sanchez. The five of us were together on our research vessel. We were attacked. I was knocked unconscious, and, when I woke up, she was missing. I don't know if anybody else saw what happened to her." She glanced around at the others.

They all shook their heads.

"So what you're saying is, the four of you were brought down here but not the fifth?"

"It's possible they killed her," Vanessa said. "I don't know. She was always feisty, and they might have hit her a little too hard to stop her from fighting back." The thought was so painful she'd refused to consider it earlier.

"Anything's possible," Jasper said. "But the rest of us are damn glad to see you. That storm caught us locked down below. With no pilot steering this thing, going through that storm tossed us around aimlessly, making for a bad night."

"I hear you," Vince said. "I skirted the storm, trying to get here as soon as possible. We're stocked with supplies, but we'll tow this vessel back if we can. Otherwise, she'll end up as ocean debris." Then again he knew it would slow them down. And might put them in trouble with fuel. He faced her. "Where were you on the research ship when you were taken?"

She ran her fingers through her hair, finding it drenched in saltwater and sticky with blood. She pulled her fingers back and winced. "We were working on board the research vessel. Dr. Sanchez had been on shore early that morning. When she got back in with the last of the day's data and the last of the equipment, she said she wasn't feeling well and went to lie down. I didn't see her after that."

"After she was on board, we moved deeper into the ocean's waters to gather more underwater data and were just about done. I was working in the ship's lab, the research bay. I remember turning around at a noise and found the kidnappers already there, holding rifles on me. I jumped to my feet, but they overpowered me." Her voice trembled. She firmed up and continued, "When I woke up, we were in the hull of this old boat, tied up and gagged."

The men were asked the same questions, but they all had variations of the same event. They hadn't come prepared to fight so had been easily taken.

In fact, as she thought about it, taking them captive had been easy—too easy.

VINCE STUDIED THE four of them. "Any idea why Dr. Sanchez would have been separated from the rest of you?"

The others shook their heads.

"She was from a wealthy family," Vanessa said. "If she was taken somewhere else and isn't dead, then maybe …" She shrugged. "I don't know if the kidnappers were trying to get a ransom for her or not. Honestly, as to our research vessel, the kidnappers probably would have done better trying to get ransom money for all of us *and* the ship from our government."

"No," Dr. Walker said. "The US has a history of not negotiating with pirates for hostages."

Vanessa frowned at him. "That's hardly fair," she snapped.

"Doesn't matter if it's fair or not," he said. "Bargaining for something like that has no end."

Vince agreed, but that didn't mean they would leave this other woman behind. Vince's first priority was making sure Vanessa was fine. "Are you hurt or injured?"

She shook her head. "Jasper was conked over the head pretty hard. He was the last of us to wake up. The rest of us seem to be fine. We were locked in down there. The kitchen is there, so we had fresh water and food. Once we overwhelmed one attacker, the other one came down, but then he must have sensed something was wrong because he backed up, closed and locked the hatch door. We never heard anything more from him. But we didn't see another boat either, so I don't know what happened to him."

"Do you think he would have jumped?" Johan asked. "Maybe he decided to leave you guys alone and just took his chances swimming to shore?"

The others all shook their heads.

"There was no point," Vanessa stated. "He could have lifted the hatch door and opened fire, but he didn't do that. As a matter of fact, I suspect he could have unloaded his machine gun into the floor of the deck above us and killed all of us without even knowing where we were. ... That is a chilling thought. Why didn't he do that?"

Vince had no idea and ignored her last question. "So another boat? Or did he have a lifeboat here?"

"I guess that's possible," Vanessa said to answer his question. "We didn't hear another motor boat, but he might have had a Zodiac he could have unloaded and used to get to another boat, leaving us all alone."

"The thing is, why would they leave us alone?" Dr. Walker asked. "Wouldn't they have come back after us?"

"They could just be keeping an eye on us," Tony said, turning to Vince, a question in his eyes.

Vince shook his head. "We saw nobody else on the ocean. Granted, the first part we spent in the storm, so there was no seeing much of anything. But, after the storm passed, we've had no sightings of other ships or boats in this area."

"Well," Tony continued, "you know we wouldn't have survived for too long. Not much fresh water was down there.

Give us a week, ten days. The kidnappers could come back then, open up the hatch, find us all dead, toss our bodies in the sea and retake the ship. It's not like they didn't know where we were."

Vanessa shook her head, seemingly in deep thought again. "This boat was not anchored, not the way it was tossed about in the storm, going for long stretches in one way until it twisted in another direction. And, given the storm, this boat is probably nowhere near where the kidnappers left us."

"But the kidnappers must have had some purpose for taking you in the first place," Johan said. "Do you have any idea what it is?"

Everyone shook their heads.

"But why didn't they just kill us when they first boarded the research ship?" Vanessa asked, not really expecting an answer, just formulating her thoughts while staring at the floor. "They were armed. They were brutal enough." Then her head popped up to focus on her rescuers. "I presume you guys think the research ship is still in this area, right? And that there have been no ransom demands for the ship or for any of our team members either, correct?" At their nods, she continued, "If the kidnappers weren't taking the research ship to resell or for their own purposes, and they weren't ransoming us or the ship off for money, why go to the trouble to move us at all? Again, I ask, why didn't they just kill us immediately?"

Vince studied them. "Because they didn't want to stir up an international event and wanted only the other doctor?"

Vanessa looked at him. "That's two scary thoughts." She frowned. "But, even so, why not kill us on this boat and leave our dead bodies here for the storm and the sea to finish off? We'd never be found again. International crisis could never be proven and thus would be averted."

Johan said, "Because they wanted to hide you, still alive, for a while? Or hide your bodies permanently at sea, with no bullet wounds to lead back to them and their guns."

That caused Vanessa to shudder. "Regardless of these questions that just won't leave me alone, one thing seems certain. Considering Dr. Sanchez is the only one of my team not here, it's very possible the gunmen *only* wanted her."

"What was she like?"

"She *is* a sweetheart," Vanessa snapped. "I refuse to talk about her as if she's already dead."

"I didn't mean that," Vince said defensively, holding up his hand. "Just calm down. We're trying to figure out what's going on here."

"Well, I personally would like to get onto your boat," Dr. Walker said, "and go home."

"We can't leave her," Vanessa said in outrage. "She wouldn't leave you alone."

Dr. Walker shoved his hands in his pockets. "Maybe," he said with fatigue in his voice. "But we have no idea where she is or who's taken her or why. So how the hell do you expect to find her?"

"The same way these guys found us." She turned to Vince. "How did you find us?"

"We came in the direction of your last-known location," he said calmly. "We were looking for your research ship and happened to find this boat first."

"So by accident." Dr. Walker sneered. "That's helpful."

"Hardly an accident," Johan said, directing an insolent glare at Dr. Walker. "We did come to the right area. Now, if we can find your original vessel, that would tell us if she's on board with the kidnappers."

"It's possible," Vanessa said. "Our research vessel is worth millions of dollars. It's a hell of a lot better than this one."

"And, of course, on the black market, it's worth a lot more money too," Vince said with a nod. "We'll take you to our rig, and we'll contact our boss to find out what they might see from current satellite data, now that the storm has cleared this area. There must be a way to track your boat. I'm sure you have some tracking system on it."

"We ran into a storm," Tony said. "Some of our systems were disabled."

"Or were disabled for us," Vanessa said, her voice hardened. "Maybe we were targeted right from the beginning. I don't know. It just makes me very angry that poor Laura isn't here too."

"Whether she's here or not," Dr. Walker said, "the least we can do is save ourselves."

Vanessa turned to glare at him. Her disgust was evident.

Vince already didn't like Dr. Walker. Neither did Vanessa, but she remained so passionate and still had so much anger even after two days of captivity. He wondered where she had gotten so much spirit. Certainly not from George, who seemed very calm and placid. Vanessa was the opposite. She used her hands when she spoke; her facial expressions twisted and changed with everything she said. She was so animated that it was a joy to watch.

She turned to Jasper. "You have any ideas?"

He looked at her in surprise. "No, why would I?"

"Because you've been working under her for the last year. Do you have any idea why she would be targeted?"

He shook his head, a frown pulling his eyebrows together in the center of his forehead. "No," he said, "I don't. She isn't from America though. Would that make any difference?"

Vanessa said, "She's Colombian, although I'm not sure that makes a difference."

Jasper added, "She worked at the university, but she was from Colombia originally."

At the name of her birth country, Vince felt a sock to his stomach. "That can bring another whole twist into this event. What's her full name? We'll run a search on her, see if somebody in the family has contacted them asking for ransom money."

"When anybody thinks of Colombia," Dr. Walker said, "their mind immediately goes to drugs and drug cartels. Chances are, this has absolutely nothing to do with that."

"Maybe," Johan said. "But *this* is a missing person, one Dr. Sanchez. If you were the one missing, we'd be looking for you. So, until we know she's not alive, we'll go on the assumption that she is." His phone rang, and he stepped away from the group to answer it.

"What does that mean?" Dr. Walker barked to one and all. "Take us back to the mainland. We can take flights home and get our lives back together again. You can mount a rescue mission for Dr. Sanchez, if you want," Dr. Walker said in exasperation, "but the rest of us would like to go home where we belong."

Vanessa bounced forward. "Speak for yourself. Not me. I'm not leaving her alone."

"Good for you. Doesn't make a damn bit of difference to me. You can stay here and die if you want, but I want to go home," Dr. Walker shouted. "This is not my world. It's not how I want to live. It's nothing I'm comfortable with. I just want to go home to my family."

Vince understood how this wasn't everybody's kind of life. And, if Vince had a wife and kids, it would make it that much harder to stay away from them. "I hope as soon as we get the message out that we found you four, we'll get more information. If your vessel is somewhere close by, we'll find it. There is, indeed, a lot of money involved, a lot of research data involved, and a lot of people want to see that all is retrieved and back in the hands of its rightful owners."

Dr. Walker seemed to collapse in on himself. "Fine. But could we get to your boat please? This one has a ton of bad memories."

Vince nodded. "Absolutely. Come on. Let's get you guys over there. If anybody needs medical supplies, we have some with us."

Johan rejoined them. "We found your vessel. It's only a few nautical miles from here. Satellite isn't picking up anyone on board at this time, but that doesn't mean it's empty."

"Then we'll go see," Vince said. "It's close, and, if several of you are okay to pilot it back to port, then we should try to reclaim it."

On that note, Vince carefully moved them all from one boat to the other. They also had an injured man to carry over. That was tricky, but Vince and Johan managed it. And when that was done, hating too, but knowing they to, they cut the rope and let the old research vessel go. He'd snagged the GPS coordinates to send to the local government officials to track—if they cared.

Otherwise, she would bounce around in the waves for another ten years before somebody put her to good use. He was kind of sorry it wouldn't be him. She had the looks of a boat that had survived a long time and had lived through a lot of assholes.

Chapter 5

V ANESSA WATCHED FROM the bow of the boat as they
approached her research vessel. It floated as pretty as
can be on the waves. That made no sense for the kidnappers
to leave it behind, but she wasn't about to argue. She was
just so damn glad to see this ship. She'd tried to avoid
thinking about all the data they'd procured and other
research materials they had with them before being kidnapped. Surely most had been backed up, but what hadn't
been?

That was what had twisted her around sideways with
worry.

And her missing friend, of course. Her deepest fear was
that they'd get to the research ship and find her lifeless body
discarded below deck somewhere, uncaring of the precious
life they'd snuffed out so callously.

If they'd treated Laura as roughly as they'd treated
Vanessa, it was all too likely they could have killed her in the
process, even accidentally.

With Johan piloting, they sidled up to the larger research
ship. She itched to jump on board and race to the lab, but
Vince was adamant she wasn't going with him.

Tony stepped up beside her, his voice low and said,
"They make me feel bad."

Startled, she looked at him. "In what way?"

She watched the wave of embarrassment flush over his cheeks. "They are so capable," he admitted. "I'm a man too, but I can't do what they are doing. Not in a million years could I even pretend to be as capable, as macho as they are."

"Does that matter?" She kept her voice down so the others, particularly Dr. Walker, who'd make fun of Tony, couldn't hear. "Not all males can be alphas. That would defeat the logic of the term. And the world needs betas. We need the researchers and the steady forward-marching males like you," she added with a smile, slipping her arm through his. "They are who they are, and you are who you are. Rejoice in the difference of being you."

He chuckled and squeezed her arm. "Thank you for that."

She pointed Johan out as he jumped onto their research ship. "At least now Vince has backup if he needs it."

Her team was assembled on the deck of the older boat, slightly hidden, as they'd been ordered, so as not to make them easy targets. They collectively stared at the ship. Not even a shadow moved on board the research ship as the men approached. Even with Vince's arrival, she had heard no sound coming from the ship.

Why kidnap the team and leave the most valuable physical item behind?

Of course, that brought her back to the fact that, if the kidnappers had left this basically new research ship behind, then they didn't want it. What they wanted was what they had already seized—the team. But not the whole team. Likely just the missing member.

Dr. Laura Sanchez.

VINCE SWEPT THROUGH the top deck, then sent an all-clear notice to Johan. As soon as he arrived, Vince would go below, but, in this situation, backup was always a good idea.

Hearing Johan's light *thud*, announcing his arrival on deck, Vince gave the signal and slowly descended to the lower level. He moved as silently as he could, crouching to see who might be waiting for him. Even with his best efforts, the floorboards on the stairs squeaked. Weapon out, at the bottom of the stairs, he did a search of the first room.

Empty.

Nerves on high alert, with Johan slipping behind him, he searched each room, one at a time.

Nothing.

He turned to Johan, a question in his eyes.

Johan shook his head. "Obviously they didn't want the ship. Or planned to collect it later."

"That means then, they were after the crew. And likely just one member."

Exchanging grim looks, they returned to the deck. "It's empty," Vince called across. "So Tony and Jasper, come on over here with me, and we'll travel back in tandem."

It took only a few minutes to get everyone organized.

Vince laughed as Vanessa joined him on the research vessel only to disappear underneath.

Obviously she had her priorities. The guys ran through an engine check, and, hearing the powerful motor start, a cheer went up from both vessels.

Chapter 6

I T HAD TAKEN long hours to get here, but they were all back in port and pulled up at the marina.

Vanessa had spent the bulk of the time saving the work that hadn't been saved before being kidnapped. She figured the only reason to take them off the research vessel was to stop anyone from finding them. Yet, the research ship was easy to locate with its high-tech equipment.

That the kidnappers hadn't damaged anything on board was a miracle as well. It had taken her hours to get all their work to the point of shutting down the project here. She'd hoped to send a backup of all their data to cloud storage, but the weather wasn't cooperating, and she'd been forced to manually copy a full backup to disks and USB keys. If the weather permitted, the scheduled backup could still happen, but she wasn't taking any chances on losing her work.

She sat on the dock, watching as their hostage was loaded onto a gurney. The local police had been less-than-friendly over the incident until a few favors had been called in to ease the explanations.

She chewed on her bottom lip, her arms crossed over her chest, as the kidnapper was loaded into an ambulance. She hated that she felt guilty. He certainly had no intention of leaving her alive, and yet, she had left him alive. Maybe not by much though.

Jasper stood at her side. Guilt made deep furrows into his face.

"We didn't have much choice," she said in a low voice for at least the third time.

"I know," he said. "That doesn't make me feel any better."

It didn't make her feel any better either. She rubbed her temples. "I want to find Dr. Sanchez."

"Good luck with that," Jasper said. "Those men were probably after her, and they didn't want any of us tagging along. Poor Laura. Dr. Sanchez, I mean."

"Maybe," Vanessa said. "I really like her. She's been there for me over some tough years, and she's not the kind to stab you in the back. Instead, she's always got a hand out to help. I just think what it would be like if it was me alone out there. I'd want somebody to rescue me. I get that the others want to leave, and that's fine. No way I'm leaving her out there alone."

"And again, I don't think you'll have that choice," Jasper said sadly. "There's no sign of her."

Just then the two men strode up beside them. "We have a vehicle coming to take you guys to the airport," Vince said. "There isn't much in the way of a consulate here, but, if that's what you want to do, you can also go there."

Vanessa jutted her chin out. "I want to go after Dr. Sanchez."

Vince's eyebrows rose. "Yeah, that's not happening. We need skilled people—skilled in *our* line of work—not someone who is likely to get kidnapped again. Our job was to rescue you. Now that that's completed, we've decided we're going after Dr. Sanchez."

She snorted. "When you took this assignment, you

didn't even know she was missing."

"No," he admitted. "We didn't. And that makes it worse. We only knew about you four team members."

Her brows furrowed. "There were actually six. One left early, obviously the lucky one," she said almost bitterly. "Dr. Sanchez was still here with us."

"But she was supposed to leave," Jasper reminded her. "She changed her plans last minute."

"Did Dr. Sanchez replace the one who left?"

Vanessa shook her head. "There was a mix-up based on a series of paperwork issues. She decided not to risk the rest of her research trip so stayed to finish her part."

"The paperwork mix-up is likely why we were confused as the number of people on your team," Johan said. He glared at her. "We need you to go to the airport now. Our job was to return you to the mainland safe and sound. Please contact your father. We already contacted our boss to let him know we've completed the job."

There was just something off about thinking of her as a *job*. She understood these men had a job to do, and they had done it. But it still felt wrong to consider her in that light. "And who'll pay your wages to go after Dr. Sanchez?"

The two men looked at each other and shrugged. "We'll probably do it pro bono," Vince said. "We do a certain amount of jobs like that every year anyway, so this just happens to be another one." In a cool voice, he continued, "We don't do this for the money. We're both ex-military. When we left the military, we decided to continue being of service. This is what we do."

She was ashamed of her comment. "I'm sorry." She ran her fingers through her tangled hair. "I have no excuse except I'm worried about Laura. Here we are safe and sound, some of us ready to fly home—where we can have hot showers and see our families and sleep in a real bed again—but Laura could be in horrible danger. For all I know, she's already been raped and tortured." Her words were bitter. "She was the only other woman on board. It's hard for me to ignore her plight."

"We're not ignoring her plight," Vince said, "but you're not equipped to come with us."

She crossed her arms over her chest. "I could take our research vessel."

"No, you can't," Dr. Walker snapped. "It's not yours. And a lot of money is tied up in that vessel. It's not a simple case of you just hopping on board and going. There's paperwork required, and grant money needed. It's extensive. We never get enough grant money to cover the days as it is."

She turned on him. "No way we can let Laura be out there like this. We have to go after her."

"*We are* going after her," Vince reiterated.

Just then a vehicle drove up. Vince ushered everyone over and loaded the little luggage they had. But not everybody could go because the vehicle was too small.

Vanessa snorted. "I'll take the second ride. These guys can all go back on their own." And she walked toward the research craft. She called back, "Besides, I still have to lock down and wait for the next crew to come and take this ship away again. Because of what happened, we're being moved, but another crew is coming on board," she said. "I'm not leaving it."

In her cabin, she realized she still hadn't even packed. She'd been so focused on Laura and rescuing all their work that she hadn't thought about the need to pack. Obviously they were leaving right away. Although technically their original flights didn't leave until tomorrow. She just couldn't think of leaving without Laura. Vanessa didn't go on a trip like this already thinking about losing a valuable member. Particularly in these dodgy circumstances.

She packed, pondering the strange turn in her life. There were financial costs of changing their flights and renting a sleeker faster boat to search for Laura. Hotels, food, etcetera.

Just then Vince came down the gangway and sat across the berth from her. "Now what are you thinking about?"

"Your boat is too slow," she said bluntly. "So is this one. These are not meant to sail the high seas or to go after pirates. We need something faster."

"There is no *we* about it," Vince said in exasperation.

"What if I could get us a small racing yacht?" She was thinking fast. Trying to find a way forward.

"Then there's a good chance that small yacht could get lost out in the Pacific Ocean," he said. "I highly doubt you have that kind of money."

"No," she said, "I don't. But maybe someone I know does, like somebody from the global research community."

"Besides, it would have to already be down here to be of any value. A yacht stateside won't help much."

She grinned, held up her finger. "True, but I just remembered. Someone, with a yacht, is down here somewhere. I know he's on a business trip right now, but he's planning on a sailing holiday in a couple weeks, so the yacht is available in the short-term. If I could reach him ..."

"Regardless, if we took it, even with his permission or blessing," Vince said, "it could still end up being destroyed in the process."

She glared at him. "We have to do something. I can't take this research vessel. It's not mine. The one that you used to rescue us isn't yours either, and it's too slow."

"We know that." Vince snagged her hands, stilling them. "We're looking into options. But we won't go out on a search blind. There's a very good chance Laura is here in town or already in a different part of the world. We take action when it makes sense."

She nodded. "I know." And suddenly she was just so tired. She'd gotten no sleep and, now that her safety was no longer an issue, was fully focused with worry for her friend. It kept fraying at the edges of her psyche. "I don't know what to do," she murmured. "It's so damn unfair."

He nodded and tapped the palms of her hands.

She stared down at the half-moon crescents she'd dug in as she had clenched her fingers together. She sighed and tried to relax. "It's nothing compared to what it could have been. If you hadn't rescued us, you know we would be dead by now."

"No," he said. "You could have lasted at least three more days in there. Somebody would have found you."

She shook her head. "I don't know about that. It seems to me that I didn't have many options left."

"It may seem like that, but we've rescued you, so you can forget about that part of it."

"I can't forget about it," she said harshly. "Not while Laura is out there."

"We're not asking you to forget about *her*," he said. "You're not equipped, and you're not skilled for this."

Her bottom lip trembled. To her shame, she realized she would burst into tears. She stood, stiffening her spine. "Then take off," she snapped, "and let me know exactly what happens and when. I want her back here. Do you hear me?" she ordered.

He gave her the gentlest of smiles. "You know something? I don't believe we'll be following any orders you give. But nice try."

She stared at him, bewildered. "I don't get it. You have no idea where she even is."

"No," he said, "but I do have lots of team members working on this. I'm not rushing out there until I know where she is. When I know where she is, we'll go get her back."

She sagged in place. "I can stay on the research vessel for two more days. They were our scheduled days anyway. Although the next crew is coming to take possession of it, I doubt they'll be here today or tomorrow, particularly if I tell them that I'm staying to look after it."

"Why would you do that?" he asked.

Her gaze narrowed. "So I can see you bring Laura back."

He smiled. "You must care for her."

"Absolutely," Vanessa said. "She's a terrific woman. She's older than I am by at least fifteen years, but she's been a mentor for me and, in many ways, almost a mother. After my mother died, she has been the closest thing I had. I can't stand to think of her suffering in this way." The tears came to the corner of her eyes. She brushed them away impatiently. "Get her back for me, please."

"You can count on it," he said gently.

VINCE HAD ABSOLUTELY no business promising her anything of the sort. But she was the kind of woman you couldn't ignore. Although he hadn't wanted to lie, and, in his heart, it wasn't a lie but a promise he might not be able to keep. That wasn't something he wanted to happen. He'd do his best, but ... life sometimes didn't turn out the way you hoped.

His phone buzzed. He checked to find a message from Levi.

Nobody has any information on the missing woman. Are you sure she's part of the team?

Yes, contact the university. Her name should be on the list of team members.

Right, Levi typed back. **Will do.**

Vince put his phone in his pocket and lifted his gaze to Vanessa.

"What's the problem?"

"Because of the kerfuffle over the government paperwork here," he said, "we're having trouble getting anybody to believe us that Dr. Sanchez is missing. Because, as far as they are concerned, she was never here in the first place."

Vanessa slumped back in her chair.

He nodded. "I know it's frustrating, but we'll sort it out."

"Somebody has to have paperwork with her name on it," she exclaimed. "The city, the university, something."

"Do you have anything? Did you bring any paperwork with you? Papers that you have to show to the city or to the harbormaster?"

She frowned; then her face lit up. "Let me see." She dashed into the lab.

He followed at a much slower pace. It was really a beautiful research vessel. It was set up for great functionality and had the latest tech on board. He stood at the doorway to the lab, amazed. "This is absolutely nothing like the old research vessel we've been using," he said with a laugh. "And that grand old boat you were held on had its own kind of beauty but in a more old-fashioned sense, like for fishing or what-not."

She turned and smiled. "No, that old boat does not quite compare to this new research ship. Yet, if I hadn't been held captive on it, I'd have loved to spend some time on her. It was almost like a ghost ship."

Vince nodded. "It was likely taken from someone years ago," he said. "I imagine the pirates have multiple vessels they can use, depending on their needs."

"You'd think so, but then why would they have cut loose from it?"

"Not sure," he said.

He had to admit it really bothered him. According to Vanessa and her team, at least one other person had closed the hatch, and the hatch had definitely been locked from the top. He suspected the kidnapper had another rowboat or power boat pulled up on the side. Once he got onto that, he just let the boats drift apart before he turned on the engine and left. With the storm, the older boat would easily have been tossed and turned in the sea, possibly sinking in the process. An easy end to the four researchers.

That brought him back to Dr. Sanchez. "How much money does she have?"

"She doesn't have much personally," Vanessa said. "But her family does. You were right. They're very much into the drug cartels, but it's been a while since we had that conversation."

He sat back and stared. "You know that changes things entirely, right?"

She shot him a glance as she sorted through the paperwork in front of her. "Why?"

"They may have picked her up to take her back to Colombia. For all you know, it could be warring drug cartels from each side."

"She walked away from that life over ten years ago," Vanessa said. "No way they would drag her back into it."

"You've got to think about this. What if they needed her back home as a power play? She wouldn't have a choice if they threatened to kill her family. Maybe that's the whole reason all of you were attacked. It's not like they took anything. They didn't even take this expensive high-tech research ship."

She's straightened slowly and studied his face. "So you think this was all to do with her brother?"

"Who is her brother? I'm not sure I understand the dynamics here," he said.

"Her brother is the head of the family. He's a very powerful man," she explained. "I know Laura was afraid of him. She refused to go home, preferring to live at the university with her research and the students."

"But he might have needed her to go home."

"What does that mean in terms of trying to find her?"

"I think we don't need to rush out to the deep blue sea yet," he said slowly. "Maybe send out some feelers in Colombia to see if she returned home again."

"She'd still need rescuing," Vanessa pointed out.

There was almost a challenge in her voice, as if she expected him to travel to Colombia and track this woman down. He realized that, from her point of view, since she'd been rescued, so, of course, Dr. Sanchez would be. He didn't think it would be anywhere near as easy as that.

He also wasn't sure he was the right person for the job if that was the case. He had zero experience with Colombia. Whereas he knew that Merk, Stone and Swede had done several jobs there.

His fingers tapped the lab table as he thought about the options. Then he picked up the phone and sent Levi several text messages with the information she'd just given him. Levi's answer came back with several question marks, nothing but question marks. Vince responded with **Yes, check the family and the village to see if anybody's sighted Dr. Sanchez yet. Apparently the family's big enough, wealthy enough, and her brother is the big cartel boss so that there should be some media announcement about it.**

I'm checking the feeds, Levi sent back. **Stay where you are.**

No problem, he said. **We're currently staying on the research vessel that we brought back to port. Vanessa is staying on until the new crew arrives.**

Her father won't like that, Levi said.

Good luck trying to convince her to change her mind, Vince sent back. When he was done, he looked up to find Vanessa studying him curiously. He raised an eyebrow. "What?"

"You're grinning," she said. "I hardly find anything in this situation to smile about."

And he realized he really was grinning like a fool. "Sometimes we need to find a little bit of humor to lighten up an ugly situation," he pointed out. "That doesn't make it wrong."

She nodded.

Just then someone hollered outside the ship. "Hi. Anyone here?"

Vince called up to answer Johan. "I'm down here in the lab."

Within a few minutes Johan joined them. He walked

around the lab of the research vessel and whistled several times. "Talk about state-of-the-art. This is nice." He frowned and then turned to Vince. "It makes absolutely no sense why the pirates didn't take this ship."

"Except for the fact that it's an American vessel," Vanessa suggested. "It belongs to the university. Once the pirates kidnapped and killed Americans, they are engaging the entire US government. Do they want that kind of headache?"

Vince wasn't sure about any of that. He filled in Johan with the update on Dr. Sanchez's family scenario.

At that, Johan stopped midstride. "Colombian drug lords, for real?"

Vince turned to Vanessa.

"All I know is what I told you," she confessed. "The last thing I heard from her was that she hadn't been home in a long time and had no intention of ever going home."

"While she was on American soil, it might have been a little harder for them to kidnap her." He focused on Vanessa. "How often does she come on these research trips?"

They both watched Vanessa wince. "This is her first time."

At that, they both looked at each other and nodded. "So this was much more likely a snatch-and-grab to take her back home again. Her life is quite likely in danger," Johan said. "But hardly from the high seas."

Chapter 7

VANESSA HATED TO hear their newest theory. She hadn't even considered Laura's life might be in danger by leaving the US. But it did make a twisted kind of sense. She hadn't had many discussions with Laura about her family. She was remarkably closemouthed. Then, if she did belong to a drug lord family—which, of course, she hadn't really admitted—she wouldn't want everybody to know about that. And, if her life was in danger, it explained why she had not traveled much. "Why would she have come on this trip then?" she asked suddenly.

"You said there was a mess-up in the paperwork, so we're not even sure she was supposed to come, correct?"

She thought about that. "I don't know how all the mess-ups started. And I'm still looking for paperwork to confirm her part as my team. But I suppose, in a way, her brother could easily have just plucked Laura from here, taking advantage of the mix-up, and nobody could prove she had been here." She shook her head. "No, of course not. We had the paperwork. Surely the university has a copy if I can't find one here. Laura's expected back at the university. When she doesn't arrive, you know they will act."

"Maybe," Vince said. "But, for all you know, she handed in her notice before she left. Maybe she wanted to return home, or maybe she was coming here to disappear altogether."

Vanessa groaned. "Okay, as conspiracy theories go, this is getting wilder and wilder."

"They have a tendency to do that," Johan said, chuckling. "But the bottom line is, we need to delve into Dr. Sanchez's life. As soon as we figure out what she was up to herself, we'll have an idea whether she was trying to escape a situation that was about to get ugly or if she fell into a situation that's about to get uglier."

"None of this is reassuring." Vanessa walked to the rear of the lab, got her laptop, brought it to the lab table and sat down. "While we're in port, I should do some research on her. Talk to some of my friends, see what they might know. She did date another professor I know quite well. He might be a good source of information." She brought up her email, searched through and found Chaz's contact info. She sent him an email, asking if he had heard from Laura, and did he have any idea about her family or future plans she had.

His response came back fairly quickly with **What are you talking about?**

She groaned. "He's acting like he doesn't know anything." She repeated the question, saying that they were looking for her here in the Galápagos. They'd all been kidnapped, and everybody had been rescued but Laura.

This time when the response came, she tapped the table. "He's not being very forthcoming."

"Give us his name. We'll get Levi or Ice on his case. Even the local cops wherever he lives could loosen up his tongue."

She raised her gaze, startled. "Do you guys have that kind of influence?"

They both nodded. "Absolutely."

At their direction, she emailed the professor's email and phone number to both Levi and Ice.

"Now that we've done that," Vince said, "who else would know anything about her? Does she have any family in the States? Does she have any other former boyfriends? Does she have any close friends? Children?"

"No family, no children," she said. "There were a couple men she dated, that I know of, this professor being one, but I think he's an ex now. I'm not sure if she has a current boyfriend or not."

They pressed her with more questions, but she didn't have any more answers.

"Who gave permission for her to come on this trip?"

"The head of the marine department," Vanessa said. "I was asked who I wanted on the team, and I suggested eight names. I've got four of those I chose."

"Who did you not want?"

She hesitated. "Do I have to say?"

"Dr. Walker by any chance?" Vince asked in a dry tone.

She nodded. "Is it that obvious?"

"Yeah," he said. "It is obvious you two have some problems. It changes the whole dynamics of the group. Personal conflicts permeate the atmosphere."

"It's a little tough to respect somebody who's only interested in getting their ass out of town. Dr. Sanchez deserves our caring attention too."

"That's fine and dandy," Johan said, "but not if it's her Colombian friends and family who have done this. We could spend a lot of money and time searching this big bloody ocean, only to find out she'd been whisked away in the first few hours after she was kidnapped."

"She could be back home, whether she likes it or not,"

Vince added.

"That doesn't mean we ignore her or her situation," Vanessa argued. "If there was a way to get a message to her, fine. The bottom line is, we have to find out where she is."

Vince looked at her and nodded. "We do need to know that she's safe," he said slowly. "Maybe send her a message. Email or however it is you want to do it. In a way that you know she'll get it if she's anywhere close to a computer or her phone."

Vanessa looked at him in surprise. "That's a good idea. I didn't even think of it because I was thinking she was still lost out in the ocean, without her phone, like we were."

"But, if we're right, and she's in Colombia," Vince said, "this is a whole new ball game. But first we need confirmation of where she is."

Vanessa opened up an email and sent it off to her friend. She had more than one email address for her, so she sent one to all three. Then sent her a Facebook message. Then she closed her laptop and looked at the two men. "Okay, done," she said. "Now what?"

VINCE HOPED DR. Sanchez answered because it wasn't feasible to search the globe for her, so they first had to pinpoint her location. It was one thing to think the pirates had taken her off the ship, but it was another thing entirely to think her family might have taken her back to Colombia. That wasn't a good place for anybody to fool around in unless necessary. Vince didn't have a problem going to Colombia, and he had it on his list of places to see.

But he knew in his heart of hearts that going to Colombia to rescue Dr. Sanchez wasn't his job here, and he was still employed by Legendary Security. Levi had to make that call. And there was no reason for Levi to even assume Dr. Sanchez was in that kind of danger. Levi could just as easily play devil's advocate and say she was part of the kidnapping plot.

Maybe it was a way for her to disappear entirely. After all, nobody, none of the four crew members were seriously injured. And that was another point. "Because none of you were seriously injured—presuming Jasper is doing okay—some people might say she was part of the plot. That she might have had something to do with this."

Vanessa sat back. "How can you even suggest such a thing?"

Johan cut in. "Because we have to." His voice was hard. "Think about it in a rational way. She is missing. She could have gone overboard, could have been kidnapped. She could be dead or just missing on or in the ocean. For all we know, she dove into the water and drowned. The kidnappers left you all alive. The other kidnapper is gone, so you're left on board with a man you took down yourselves. Where's the logic in any of that? What does make sense is, if Sanchez arranged for this, she did so to disappear permanently."

Vince watched the anger float across Vanessa's face. She had quite a temper, this absolutely extraordinary woman. Everybody else had been more than happy to get back home again, eager to see friends and family, but not her. She was the only holdout, trying to save her friend.

"If we could hear from her that would help a lot," Vince said calmly. He squeezed her fingers. "You know law enforcement will tear this apart from the exact same angle and suggest she was a part of it too."

Vanessa shook her head. "She wouldn't have done that."

"Sure, she would have," Johan said. "We all would, under coercion or duress, in the right circumstances. She might have loved her job. She might have loved whoever it was she was currently going out with. She might have loved a lot of things in her life, but she probably loved living and breathing more. And, if her way of life was about to be put in danger, including the people she knew and loved, then she needed a way out. What better way out than this?"

"Do you remember how many pirates there were initially?" Vince asked.

Vanessa frowned. "I assumed there were a lot. I was working downstairs when we were attacked, but I only saw two gunmen at that point. I only really know that I was knocked unconscious after I was grabbed. Somebody shoved a gag in my mouth, and then I remember waking up at the bottom of the old boat."

"In other words you have no clue how many men there were. It could have been just the two you saw. And, with his partner taken out, the other guy decided to slink away. And, if you never saw the top of the old boat, and you weren't awake when you were transferred over, you have no idea what happened to Dr. Sanchez."

"I really don't want to go down that road," Vanessa replied, her voice raspy. "Do you know how hard it would be to contemplate that she had anything to do with this, that she was behind the pain and fear we experienced? Poor Jasper. His head wound is not something to be laughed at."

"Neither are the wounds on your attacker," Johan said softly. "Did she pay them? Were they cheap labor she picked up? Chances are, your attacker will never be normal again, if he even pulls through this."

Vanessa flushed. "So am I supposed to feel guilty now

for hurting him? We did what we thought we had to do to escape. And we certainly wouldn't even need to escape if those assholes hadn't kidnapped us in the first place. We did what we had to in order to save ourselves."

"Of course you had to," Vince said. "That was the only option you had. But why would they have only two armed men for the four of you?"

"Because they didn't need more," she snapped. She threw up her hands. "They were armed, remember? It's pretty hard for unarmed people, no matter how many of us, to go up against bullets."

"Did any of you have martial arts or self-defense training?" Johan asked.

Vince watched her closely.

She shook her head. "Not me. I would have sworn Dr. Sanchez was a no as well. As for the other three, I have no clue. That's anybody's guess. No, ... I take that back. Dr. Walker is a worm, a coward. So a great big no for him. Tony is gay and worried he is not an alpha male, like you two. So a no for him as well—and I'd appreciate it if you kept that fact a secret. Then there's Jasper. He may be huge, but he's a teddy bear. So no for him as well." She glanced back at Vince. "But, if you don't want my guesses, you can contact all three of them and ask them."

"We might," Vince said. He glanced over at Johan, who was studying Vanessa intently. "What do you think, Johan?"

"I think something fishy is going on here. We thought that right from the beginning. Now whether they actually planned to kill the four of you is a little premature to note until we can capture the other guy who was part of it. *If* we can capture the other guy. He's in a sea full of pirates. Who knows where he's gone to ground."

"*If* he's gone to ground," Vince said. "Because, of course, the other side of this is that somebody set it up to look like Laura might have had a part in it. In that way, if she was looking to disappear and did so successfully, they could also make her disappear successfully. And nobody would be the wiser."

Vanessa burst out, "Talk about craziness. How do you even follow the thinking in your head?"

"Easy," Vince said, hardening the tone of his voice. "Betrayal seems to go hand in hand with love."

"Or," Johan added, "betrayal comes from within a group's inner circle."

That shut her down to just quiet looks as she thought about both men's words.

Vince didn't mean to come across as a cynic—and he was pretty sure Johan would agree—but it was pretty hard not to when somebody asked the questions that she did. Particularly right now.

Still, she was doing that out of the goodness of her heart, and obviously she was worried about her friend. That was the bottom line. He could understand that. He'd been in many positions where he had been separated from a team member and had worried until they reconnected. Sometimes that reconnection had taken weeks. It depended on the type of mission and how far into enemy territory he'd gone.

He had to admire anybody so stalwart in her defense of her friend. But the more he thought about it, the more he liked the idea that maybe Dr. Sanchez had a hand in arranging this escape. If she needed to go undercover, it was a great way to do it. And then the problem became, were Vince and Johan to even try to pursue her? If they could confirm that, what were they supposed to do?

His phone rang just then. He put it on Speakerphone. "Levi, what's up?"

"Lots of things." His words held tiredness and frustration. "But nothing solid. Nobody knows anything. None of the government teams or representatives where you are have a clue who would be after Dr. Sanchez or the entire team. I doubt it's competing research companies. It's a simple process to get licenses. There isn't a ton of money involved. The research scientists have been coming for years, and the government needs their services, so they're not against them coming. They always come up with a viable plan for the local officials to implement as to how to balance tourism versus the decline of the natural habitats.

"So it's hard to imagine this issue coming from that. There's not enough money involved. The biggest local companies involved in ecotourism at Galápagos have done so for years and years, and, according to the three owners we spoke with, they didn't know anybody else trying to get in on the same industry. Only so many tourists are coming there, so one CEO said there's basically enough for the three companies and not a whole lot more.

"He did say he makes very good money off of it because the archipelago is so protected that he and his guys do everything to bring in new money streams. But they have to be strict as they still get a lot of tourists who want to leave garbage behind or who want to ride on a turtle. He said sometimes you have to really be mean. But you have to watch it too because, if you don't balance that out, then the negative reviews come, and you'll see your tourist numbers going down."

"I'm surprised they even want tourists here then, if they're being shitheads."

"It's their business. It's their lifeblood," Levi said. "That's a problem faced by many delicate ecosystems around the world. How do you balance that almighty tourist dollar with responsibility to keep the ecosystem thriving? He did suggest there was a lot of competition at the market level to supply the tourists. Although he didn't know of many pirates in the area, he had heard of some people stealing supplies before they ever made it to the market. He wasn't sure if that was the black market operating a quick switch of hands, so other people had better produce or more produce, or whether it was typical low-end finagling of stock. He said, if they can hold back shipments of, say, mangoes, for a day, by the next morning, the price of mangoes had shot up, and they could sell off their stock at a very healthy profit."

Vince looked up to see Vanessa's jaw drop at that. But he understood. "It's kind of dicey to do that," he said.

"That's basically supply and demand though, isn't it?" Levi said. "And we see it in the stock markets all the time. It's still illegal, but it won't stop anybody from doing it."

"No, it won't," Johan said quietly. "And, if you think about it, if you take something that's not quite as plentiful off the market for even two or three days, by the time it finally shows up, the profits are huge."

"Yeah, exactly." Levi's voice changed as he hesitantly said, "We're checking with the university, with friends of everybody on the team. Everybody was held in fairly high regard, and we heard there was a special relationship between Jasper and Dr. Sanchez. Can anyone confirm that?"

"I have Vanessa sitting across the table from me. What do you say to that?" Vince asked.

"They were friends," she said. "I know she thought a lot of him, thought he had the potential to go far. He was one of those genius kids who graduated early, got his first degree early, and the second degree seemed to just line up without any effort."

Vince studied her face, looking for any hint of jealousy or envy, but there was nothing. "Do you think the relationship was anything other than professor and mentor to help an amazing student?"

"I don't think there could be anything between them more than that," she said slowly. "There's been a few rumors about Dr. Sanchez and students, but no one ever reported her, so I'm sure those were just rumors." She shrugged. "People should just mind their own business."

"When you all realized Dr. Sanchez wasn't with you, who was the most shocked, and who was the least shocked?" Levi asked.

"Oh, very interesting question," Vince muttered under his breath as he watched Vanessa process what Levi was asking.

She frowned, and it was like her whole face frowned. She was very animated most of the time. He'd never seen anybody with such an expressive face.

"I think the least upset was Dr. Walker," she said in a tense tone. "But, keep in mind, he's all about himself. I think Tony was quite worried but also felt like there was nothing we could do about it, and we needed to save ourselves first."

"And what about Jasper?" Levi asked. "If they were as close as everyone believes, how devastated was he?"

"He was the one knocked out the longest," she said slowly. "He lay unconscious on the floor for a long time. When he did finally wake up, we were already going on the attack, so I'm not sure he had much time to process she wasn't there. But ..." She stopped and gave a head shake.

"No, it can't be."

"What can't be?" Levi asked.

"He didn't ask," she said in shock. "He never asked where Dr. Sanchez was. From the time he woke up ... No, I think I told him immediately, well, as soon as he was lucid, so he knew already. And then we attacked one of our kidnappers. So he didn't need to ask anything about Laura."

They could hear Levi whisper, "Bingo."

"Are you thinking he had something to do with her disappearance?" Vince asked Levi. He exchanged a glance with Johan. "We have a different theory."

"Speak up then," Levi said. "What do you think happened?"

"We were wondering if she'd arranged her own disappearance," Vince said. "If you think about the facts, the four people who were on this boat were her teammates, and no one was seriously hurt. Yes, Jasper sustained several blows to the head, and one required stitches, but, in the scope of things, it could have been so much worse. Those men had rifles. They had a lot of firepower. If they'd wanted to, they could have not only shot the victims but they could have put a hole in the boat before leaving, and it would have sunk the boat with all the team in it, never to be found again. But they didn't. So maybe the gunmen weren't pirates or kidnappers but maybe her family or some paid guns to whisk her away."

"But," Vanessa interrupted, "they left us to die on that boat. Laura would not do that."

Vince added, "Or maybe she instructed those men, after a day or two, to anonymously leave the GPS coordinates with the local authorities or the university or even with her hired goons to transport you back to safety."

"And to what purpose do you think she wanted to reinvent her life?" Levi asked his men.

"The only thing we have come up with so far, and we haven't done very much digging yet," Vince said, "is the fact she's connected to a drug cartel in Colombia."

Silence. "As a connection, that's a pretty good theory," Levi said. "I was trying to figure out if anybody had any reason to get rid of her. If Jasper and she were lovers, it's quite possible he wanted to get rid of her because she ditched him. And then he would have had something to do with it that the others didn't know about. If you were unconscious right away, Vanessa, then how do you know what conversations or actions the others all had on their own?"

"I don't," she said. "Obviously, if I was out cold, I couldn't have. I didn't really see anybody as I was attacked from behind. Then, as I turned, I saw two gunmen, mostly the two guns. When I woke up, I was tied up in the bottom of that old boat. And the other three men were with me."

"So it's quite possible that three of you were attacked the same way, and yet, they could have been on the instructions of Jasper."

"I can't believe that. He's awfully young to arrange something like that," she said. "And it's pretty ugly to even think somebody that age would want to do something like that."

"Serial killers come in all ages," Levi said coolly. "But more than that, this man is highly intelligent, is he not?"

"Yes, of course he is," she said dropping her hands on the table. "I just can't believe Jasper would be involved in either theory."

"Why not?" Levi asked.

She stared down at the phone. "Because he was the one who got beat up the most and because he's in love with Laura."

Chapter 8

V ANESSA HESITATED FOR a moment, then elaborated on
Jasper's attachment to Laura. "I'm pretty sure he was.
It's not like he ever talked about it, but he always had this
warm glow around him. And the two of them had an
obvious connection whenever they were together. We all
noticed, but none of us commented. Again they were adults.
Jasper was young and obviously a good twenty to twenty-five
years her junior, but, if it was the other way around, we
would have just raised our eyebrows and shrugged. Because
you see that happening all the time in universities. The age
difference here made some of us question it, but, at the same
time, there was no need to be worried about Jasper. He was a
healthy adult male. And, if that was the direction he wanted
to go, and she was willing, then fine."

"So we need to contact each of the team members, interview them individually," Levi said, his voice echoing oddly in
the phone suddenly. "Find out who was where and who was
attacked when and what they might have heard."

"As far as I know, they're on the way to the airport."
Johan said. "Unless that has changed."

"It has changed," Levi said. "Somebody from the university wanted to make sure nobody in their research team was,
first off, hurt and then wanted to make sure nobody pointed
the finger at the team. That they might have brought this on

through a conflict or inefficiency. So currently everybody is at a hotel. I'd like you to join them there. Instead of interviews, find out exactly how this went down and in what order everyone was taken and who saw what."

"Are we doing this in a formal way, or could we just take them out for a casual dinner and pump them for information?" Johan asked.

"Casual if possible," Vince suggested. "And then formal if we have to."

Vanessa nodded. "I can probably get the conversation going. I really do want to know what happened. If Jasper was the last one to go down, which is possible, and yet, he was beaten the worst, what did he know? What did he see? And who was the last one to see Dr. Sanchez alive?"

"That's what I'd like to know," Vince said. "And where was she when she was last seen?"

"Let's get moving," Johan said. "We don't want these people, if they are involved, trying to escape."

Vanessa got up quickly, packed up the rest of her stuff, which she had already partially packed earlier before deciding she would stay on board. She turned to look around and sighed. "I have so enjoyed my trips on this ship. I'm not sure if I'll ever get another chance to come again."

With her backpack over her shoulder and one carry-on with all her business paperwork, she loaded up her laptop and charger, grabbed the stacks of files, the storage devices that she had and shut down all the equipment still left running. With everything shut off, she walked outside on deck, joining Vince and Johan there.

"A new crew is supposed to come and take this vessel back again," she said. "I'm not sure if we're planning on wintering it or renting it out. That's the university's deal, not mine."

"We've already closed off the rest of the research vessel," Johan said as he came toward her. "It's just a matter of the three of us heading to the hotel now."

In the cab she didn't say anything, just watched as the market she'd seen many times before disappeared. She had a lot of good memories here, a few not so good as well, but there was a sense of finality to this trip. She didn't know if this craziness would stop the university from allowing these trips to happen or not. They were very expensive. The rent for these research vessels for two weeks was astronomical but made the university good money to cover the vessels' upkeep. The data they retrieved was also valuable.

They'd been coming for seven years in a row now. She knew, at some point in time, new data wouldn't give them a whole lot more information. She wanted to keep coming because she wanted to keep fighting the fight to snuff out the fierce encroachment, if not to lessen it.

When they got to the hotel, she hopped out, waited for the men to leave the cab and join her. The three walked into the reception area.

"We need their room numbers," she said, "and we should call them to go out for lunch." She checked her watch. "Make that dinner."

As they crossed the lobby, she saw Tony sitting in one of the big easy chairs out front, talking on a cell phone. She planted herself right in front of him, a big grin on her face. But she was ever watchful of his reaction to seeing her. Happily it was just joy.

He hopped up and hugged her. "I'm so glad to see you," he said. "I hated to leave you back at the docks."

"Not to worry," she said. "The three of us are here at the

hotel now. They suggested taking us out for dinner. I was thinking we should take them out for dinner. They did save our lives."

Tony agreed. "Sure. Jasper is lying down, but I don't know about Dr. Walker." He walked up to the front reception desk and waited while they all registered. He smiled when he saw their room number. "We're all on the second floor."

"Lead the way then," Johan said.

Because they had as many bags as they did, they took the elevators up. As they popped out onto the second floor, they saw Dr. Walker heading toward the elevator. There was purpose in his stride.

He came to a halt and frowned when he saw them. "What are you doing here?" he asked Vanessa.

"Wow. Hi. How are you?" she said with a sarcastic tone. "We're all fine. It's all right that you got to leave, and the men who rescued you are just now dragging in. They wanted to take us out for dinner tonight, but I suggested we should reverse that, since they saved our lives."

She knew she was putting it on a bit heavy, but, with Dr. Walker, it was hard to do anything but. The man was an ass and made her life more than a little miserable.

He hesitated.

"You surely can't have plans already," she snapped. "You just arrived."

His nose went up a notch. "As it happens, I do have plans. But I can change them." He turned to Vince and Johan. "One thing I should have done"—he held out his hand and shook each of theirs—"is thank you. And, for that, I am truly sorry. At the time, all I could think about was getting back home safe and sound. And I did forget to show my appreciation."

He did it so well Vanessa was amazed. How could he turn on the charm and turn on the officiousness at will like that? It was a real skill.

He turned to her. "Of course we could take them out for dinner." He looked over at Tony. "Are you all settled in?"

Tony nodded. "I was just down in the lobby making phone calls when they walked in."

"What about Dr. Sanchez?" Dr. Walker asked. "Any word of her yet?"

Vince and Johan both shook their heads.

"Who was the last to see her?" Vanessa couldn't help asking. "When I was taken, it was just me down in the research bay. Two gunmen came after me, overpowered me, and put a gag in my mouth. Then they slammed me in the head and I was out cold." She looked up at Dr. Walker. "What happened to you?"

"I was sitting on the deck by the lifeboats," he said, "working on my papers. We had an awful lot of data that wasn't making much sense. Remember how some of the data streams were corrupted? That was when the men came up on either side of the boat. I didn't recognize either of them, but now I know one of them was the man we overpowered down below on the boat. I ran around the corner and got hit from behind. Then, like you, I woke up in that old boat."

They both turned to Tony.

He shrugged. "I was up in the pilot cabin. I was on duty that day."

Dr. Walker nodded. "Oh, yeah, you were. And you didn't see them arrive?" he asked in astonishment. And then his gaze narrowed. "And why is it you didn't see them arrive?" His tone was hard, rimmed with disbelief. "It's one thing to maybe have stowaways from shore, but surely you'd have seen them arrive."

Tony flushed.

Dr. Walker crossed his arms over his chest. "Just what the hell were you doing?" he snapped.

"I was napping," Tony snapped back. "You know very well we were up late the previous night. We were trying to figure out why the equipment was giving us such a hard time. I went to bed around three. Sitting up there in the hot sun, we were trying to conserve fuel, so it's not like I was running the air-conditioning," he said sarcastically. "I put my feet up on the counter and closed my eyes."

"Okay, so hang on a minute," Vince said. "Where was their boat?"

Dr. Walker and Tony both turned to look at him in confusion. "What boat?"

"Where did they come from? How did they arrive at your research vessel?" Johan asked. "I presume they didn't just get helicoptered in and drop from the sky."

Dr. Walker shook his head. "I have no idea. I didn't hear a boat either until they were right there." He frowned at that. "But I should have, shouldn't I?" He turned to Vanessa. "Did you hear anyone?"

She shook her head. "But again, I was down below. I didn't hear a boat arrive, and I didn't hear anybody even come down the damn stairs. I had my headset on."

He rolled his eyes at that. "You always insist on music when you work. Why is that?"

She sighed. "Because it blocks out all the noise so I can work better. Lots of people wear headphones or headsets during work."

They turned to look at Tony.

"So you had no warning?" Vanessa asked in disbelief. "I know the research vessel is big, but you couldn't see anything on either side?"

He shook his head. "I was thinking about that earlier. I figure they must have come up behind, and then, as soon as they boarded, I was probably the first one taken out. And, like I said, I was napping. I'm the one who should have seen them," he said regretfully. "But I didn't, and, for that, I'm very sorry."

"Well, *sorry* hardly helps now, does it?" Dr. Walker sighed. "I guess it doesn't make much difference either since we're all safe."

A stillness settled on the group.

Vanessa turned ever-so-slowly to look at Dr. Walker. "But we aren't *all* safe, are we? We're missing Laura. What do you know that we don't?" she asked. "Because someone has to know something. And, if not us, then Jasper."

"I don't know anything," Dr. Walker said. "I just meant we're all safe now that we're here. I don't know anything about Dr. Sanchez." At that, he shut up.

"IN THAT CASE, we better find Jasper and ask him some questions, hadn't we?" Vince said, keeping his voice light.

Was Dr. Walker just an asshole? Or was he more involved in all of this than anyone knew? Vince couldn't imagine how the team's families would feel if they found out this entire ploy was for this woman to just disappear on her own. Or if someone on board had a reason to make this woman disappear.

A lot of families had been brokenhearted over this event. Sure, the kidnapping itself for these four team members had only been a couple days long. But that didn't make it any less traumatic. He glanced over at Tony. "Any idea which room Jasper is in?"

He nodded. "He is in the one between the two of us but on the other side." He motioned at Dr. Walker and looked down the hallway. "It's that one." He pointed. "His headache was killing him. He said he would lie down."

Dr. Walker tilted his nose in the air. "That head injury isn't to be trifled with."

"No, it wasn't," Vanessa said gently. "Did either of you think to look in on him? Keep an eye on him to make sure he doesn't have a bleed in his head?"

Tony looked at her in horror, then glanced at the door again. "I never even thought of that." He turned back to Dr. Walker. "Was the injury that bad?"

Dr. Walker shrugged. "I didn't look at it." Then, as if being dismissed, he looked at his watch. "When do you want to go out to eat? I'm quite hungry now."

Vince looked at his watch. "We'll check on Jasper first. How about in an hour?"

Dr. Walker's lip curled. He finally nodded. "Fine. I'll go to the bar and have a drink and wait." He walked past them.

Vince glanced at Vanessa, who glared at Dr. Walker's retreating back. "He can be such a conceited, arrogant asshole," she muttered as he entered the elevator.

Tony chuckled. "And you love him anyway," he said affectionately. "He brings in a ton of grant money that allows all of us to keep our jobs."

Her shoulders sagged. "True enough." She walked toward Jasper's door.

Vince stayed right beside her. As he looked over at Tony, then at Vanessa, he said, "So you two aren't doctors?"

"We both are, but we're scientists not medical doctors, so PhDs not MDs," Tony said. "And the titles don't really matter to us. I don't care if somebody calls me formally by my title or not."

Vince looked over at Vanessa. "And you?"

She glanced at him with a frown. "What do I care? It adds cache to the papers I write and validates my work, but I'd much rather people understand the work I do than the title I carry."

He grinned at her. "I kind of like that attitude."

She shot him a look. "Well, it's obvious you're crazy. Or you just like crazy women," she muttered half under her breath.

He heard her anyway. "I've decided I like women with spirit."

"That's probably because you've been around doormats all your life." She snorted. "The last thing I am or ever will be is a doormat."

"I don't think I've been with anybody who was a doormat," Vince said. "But I have definitely not met too many women like you."

"Maybe it's just the circumstances." She then rapped on Jasper's door sharply. When there was no answer, she rapped again. Frowning, she looked back at Vince. "Now what?"

Vince turned toward Tony. "When did you see him last?"

"When we arrived. Other than that, there's been no contact between any of us. I have to admit, I was feeling kind of out of sorts. That's why I was down in the lobby. I didn't want to be alone. Being alone on that damn ship was enough for me for a long time. And, of course, I wasn't totally alone. But I was the one who woke up first. And it took a long time for the others to come out of their grogginess to join me. It was the most incredibly lonely, isolated feeling," he said soberly. "I just didn't want to be isolated anymore, so I was sitting in the lobby, waiting for time to pass. I'd hoped to fly out tonight, but it's not happening apparently."

"No, definitely some questions have to be asked."

Tony nodded, grumbling. "And yet, it's the same questions. Like, *Who did this to us?*" he said passionately. "What about the guy we took down? Is he okay? Has anybody asked him any questions?"

Johan said, "You know what? That's a very good point. I'll contact the authorities and see if they can give us an update." He stepped a few feet away and made a call.

He was far enough away they could not hear the conversation.

Just to make sure, Vince walked up to Jasper's door and gave it a really hard pounding. "Jasper, you in there?"

"There's no way to know if he's even inside?" Vanessa asked.

"He's a big guy. He could have gone down to the market and sat outside, and nobody would bother him," Tony added. "He's quite comfortable in all parts of the world, and he's very much an explorer, so going to the market would be right up his alley."

Vince considered that and realized, for anybody who wanted to travel the world, staying in a hotel for so many hours was hardly what they would want to do. "Actually that makes a lot of sense." He looked at the sky through the end of the hallway window. "It is a nice day out."

"Maybe we should check at the front desk and see if he's left," Tony said. "They should know."

"No, they won't," Vanessa said. "Why would they? Unless he stopped to ask for directions, they won't notice if yet another hotel guest walks in and out of the door."

"Except how many guests are six-five and 280 pounds?" Vince asked.

"You've got a point there," Johan said, chuckling.

Tony slipped his hands into his pockets and rocked on his heels. "Regardless it is one avenue to check. If we're worried about him, then we have to get somebody to open his door. And, if he's in there sleeping, he won't be very happy with that. And, if he's not alone in there"—he waggled his eyebrows—"he'll be very, very unhappy."

"Not a sound is coming from that room," she said softly. "So I highly doubt he's picked up somebody already. I'm more concerned he's inside and has slipped into a coma."

"But we don't know that for sure he's alone," Tony said. "Remember? He always had a girl on his arm."

"Did you ever hear that he had Dr. Sanchez on his arm?" Vince asked suddenly.

Tony looked at him in surprise. "I heard rumors. But I think that's all they were, just rumors."

"Why is that?" Vince asked.

"The age difference," he said. "I don't see the attraction myself, so maybe it's possible but I didn't ever see them together."

Vince nodded. "Just had to ask."

"I don't get it," Tony said. "I don't understand what the undercurrents are, but there's definitely something happening here. I understand Dr. Sanchez is missing, and we need to find her, but I'm not sure how that works."

"So far, we haven't seen anybody who's even seen her recently," Vince explained. "When did you last see her on the research vessel yourself?"

Tony frowned. "I'm not sure I saw her that day of the kidnapping at all. I was up in the pilot's cabin, like I said. I was on shift that day. I didn't see her at breakfast, so it must have been the night before."

"Did anybody check on her that evening?" Johan asked.

Vanessa shook her head. "I did, right before I went to bed. Didn't you?"

Tony shook his head. "No. Now I feel like I should have. Do we even know if she was on the ship when it was raided?"

"Is there any reason to suspect she might have tried to commit suicide?" Vince's voice was low, quiet, but he needed to bring it up. "Any chance she went overboard, and you wouldn't have noticed?"

Both stared at him in horror.

"It's possible," Tony said, "in the sense that she would have had access to the entire vessel. And it's big. But drowning is not an easy way to kill yourself. And she was an excellent swimmer. Her body would fight her totally on that."

"Absolutely," Vanessa said. "Swimmers struggle not to drown. You have to exhaust yourself."

"Or have weights you can't fight against," Vince said. "I'm not suggesting she did that, but, if you haven't seen her since early afternoon on the day you were taken—over two days ago—how do we know she was on board at the time? How do we even know she is missing? Did you have extra lifeboats on the research vessel? Were they all there when you got up that morning? Are they there now? Did you have other boats you used? Did you have other boats close by where she could have swum to?" He wondered when they both looked at him in surprise. "Think about it. What if she knew somebody in one of the other boats? How close were other people moored beside you?"

"The lifeboats are accounted for," Vanessa said. "One of us checks that each morning and each night. And it was my turn to do it, so I can confirm that issue. For both the morning of the day of our kidnapping and even now, after we reclaimed the ship."

"There was one vessel close to us," Tony said. "It was another research team. They were there for about four days. We had a couple other sailing vessels around. It's quite common when you anchor to have others close by. People are naturally sociable."

Vince nodded. "Think specifically about the night before the kidnapping and the day of the raid by the gunmen, was there anybody close to you?"

"There were three other boats," Vanessa said. "A small catamaran—somebody had been traveling around the islands. A small yacht. I don't know who was on it, but I think it was called Katia." She looked over at Tony for confirmation.

He shrugged. "We didn't keep track of anybody close to us. There was no need to. It's international waters, and people come and go all the time."

"And there's no marina at some of the more remote areas, so people anchor wherever they want to."

"And the third boat you saw?"

"It was a small cruiser," she said. "I don't know who it was. They were friendly enough. As they went past us, they waved. We did too."

"So I repeat, is it possible Dr. Sanchez left with one of them?"

"*We* don't know," Vanessa said, enunciating clearly.

"Remember? We didn't see her after we were taken from the ship. I was knocked out. For all I know, three or four other vessels were around us then. When we woke up on the old boat, we heard two men, that we knew of, walking the deck. We didn't really see the second man. We saw the first one only, and he's the one we overpowered to gain our freedom. Also, looking out the portholes, we couldn't see any other ships."

"But it's possible the remaining kidnapper had a boat he took off in."

"As far as we know, you were the only ones around us for miles. Did you see anyone close?" She turned the tables on him.

"No," he said. "There was that big storm. We avoided it, found you on the outskirts in the kidnapper's old boat, but nobody was close by."

She nodded. "So, we can't answer where our research vessel actually was at the time of the raid, especially if the storm knocked out some of our tracking systems beforehand and if our pilot at the time was asleep." She sent a sideways glance to Tony.

He must have had the proper look of shame to keep her on her original line of thought.

"When we found the research vessel again, it was empty, and nobody was close by then either."

"And that's a damn good thing," Tony said. "But it also belies the theory that we were taken by pirates, doesn't it? That vessel is extremely valuable. The equipment on it is extremely valuable. And yet, it was just floundering in the water."

"It was anchored," Vince said. "It just floated gently. It wasn't in any distress. It was completely abandoned. That's the confusing part."

"Very," Vanessa said. "It makes absolutely no sense. Not if it were truly pirates."

Vince looked at her and gave her a fat smile. "Exactly."

Just then the elevator doors opened, and a manager walked out. Seeing the group standing outside Jasper's door, he asked, "May I help you?"

"Is it possible to find out if the person in this room has left for the afternoon, for the evening," Vince asked, "or if he's still in there?"

The manager frowned at him. "We're not allowed to give out any information on our guests," he stated in a snotty tone.

Vince made a sudden hand gesture. "He has a bad head injury. Our concern is that he's in there dying."

The manager sucked in his breath noisily. "I really don't know what to do in this instance. Let me call down to the desk and see if anybody knows anything."

He moved toward the end of the hallway near the window. On his cell phone, he had a conversation they couldn't hear the details of.

When he came back he said, "No one at the front desk remembers seeing him." He motioned for them to step back. "I'll open the door. I want to make sure, if he's in there, he's either sleeping or at least okay. But I don't want any of you coming in after me." He pulled out a master key and unlocked the door, stepping inside, closing the door behind him. The door opened immediately, and he looked at them with a smile. "He's not here." He closed and locked the door again. "You can wait for your friend down in the lobby."

Vince had seen just a corner of the bedroom as the main door had opened and closed, and the bed had definitely no sign of Jasper. Confident he was out somewhere doing his thing, Vince turned to the others. "We might as well get settled into our rooms. We have time for a quick change, and then we'll go for dinner. Do any of you have a way to contact Jasper, have a cell phone number or something? If so, let's arrange for him to meet us for dinner."

"We can text him," Tony said, pulling out his phone. He sent off a text. "I should have done this in the first place."

As they stood here, they heard a funny sound from inside Jasper's room. Vanessa gasped, turned, walked over to the door. "That makes no sense."

"What's that?" Vince asked as he unlocked the door to the room he shared with Johan.

"That is Jasper's cell phone," she said. "He has a very distinctive Daffy Duck voice clip."

Vince walked back toward her. "You're right. It makes no sense. He wouldn't walk around a foreign city without his cell phone. Or did he have a work phone and a personal phone? I know plenty who do?"

"I don't know." Vanessa stared at the door in frustration. "The manager said nobody was in there. Did he give it a thorough check?"

Tony patted her shoulder. "Look. Jasper just forgot his cell. Maybe he's down having a drink. Come on. Go get changed. We'll go out for dinner, and hopefully he'll be back by the time we are finished."

They finally persuaded her, and she entered her room, locking it behind her.

Vince and Johan exchanged glances. Johan took their hotel key, popped out a different key card from his wallet and walked over to Jasper's room. Within seconds he had it unlocked.

Vince slipped in behind him. Sure enough, the cell phone sat on the night table. Jasper's unpacked bag was on the bed. It looked like his wallet was there too. That made no sense. He quickly checked it. There was no money in it, just cards, which was not so unusual in this day and age, especially when traveling. They did a search of the room, even checking under the bed, but there was no sign of him.

Frowning, they looked at each other and slipped out of the room.

In their own room, Vince said, "That makes no sense."

"No, it doesn't." Johan stood in the room, staring out the window. "He must be with somebody else then."

"That would mean Dr. Walker. But Dr. Walker was alone when we saw him."

"I was thinking Dr. Sanchez." Johan turned to face him.

Vince's eyebrows popped up. "That's possible, but nobody has seen her either."

"Do we know that? We need to get some photos and circulate them around the hotel and elsewhere."

"Good idea," Vince said as he grabbed his gear, put it on the bed and popped out his laptop. He brought up a photo of Dr. Sanchez. "I don't know if this is the most recent one, or the closest likeness, but I think it would print off well." He emailed it to himself then added it to a USB key and pocketed it. "Do you need a shower or change?"

Johan shook his head. "We haven't done anything to work up a sweat yet."

Vince laughed. "Sounds like you're almost disappointed."

"I prefer action over inaction any day," Johan said.

They exited the room, went down to the main reception desk, where Vince got several copies of Dr. Sanchez's face printed off. And then, as a secondary thought, he asked them to print off a copy of Jasper's face as well. They looked up at him when he said he needed to bring the face up on Google, but it was quick and easy with the university's website.

So, with those copies of each printed off, he turned and handed several to Vince, then turned to look at the receptionist, asking if they had seen the woman. The picture was passed around to several people nearby, but they just shrugged.

"So does that mean no, or maybe something close to that?"

One young man stood nearby. He took a look and shrugged. "I think I saw her, but it was about a week ago."

"Good," Vince said. "That would make sense. They docked here before they headed out on their annual trip. They needed supplies and stocked up from here."

"Yeah," he said. "She was with a bunch of men and maybe another woman."

Vince was encouraged to at least have somebody who had seen that much of her. "You haven't seen her since?"

The young man frowned. "I don't think so. She should be back in soon though. Come to think of it, I may have seen some of those men who were with her. But I'm not sure."

Vince thanked him, and he and Johan walked into the front lobby. Several people sat here, reading papers or busy on their phones. It seemed like, in the digital age, everybody did everything on their phones now. Vince asked a couple of them if they had seen Dr. Sanchez, but there was no recognition on any of their faces. On a hunch he walked into the pub and asked there. The bartender did recognize her, but again from a week ago.

By the time he was done, he met Johan out in the front again and shrugged. "No sign of her."

Johan said, "Nobody seems to have seen Jasper either."

"He probably came down and went straight out onto the street."

"Possibly."

They stepped out onto the street, knowing they didn't have much time before they met the others for dinner.

"The market should be still going strong," Johan said. "We can walk down one side and back up the other before we meet the others."

"Good idea. You ask about her. I'll ask about him."

They split up, going down each side, asking everybody.

When they met again at the top, they were both hot and disgusted, each shaking their heads.

"So nobody has seen either of them," said Johan.

"I could see that with Dr. Sanchez, particularly since she's not here anymore," Vince said. "But Jasper is big. It's pretty hard to not see him."

"Unless he hasn't left the hotel yet," Johan said. "I get that Dr. Walker is an asshole, but I don't know if he's also a liar."

Chapter 9

V ANESSA SENT SEVERAL text messages to Jasper, and, for the hell of it, she sent several to Laura again as well. Vanessa had no clue what was going on and could only hope Jasper was just being the typical kid, lost in his enjoyment of exploring a new place. There was a slim chance he'd return to his room to retrieve his phone. She couldn't forget he was a global traveler. Comfortable, natural and very curious in all settings.

He really was a traveler, that one. Anytime they had a place to stop, he got excited and researched all the local history so he could make the best use of his time. And maybe he'd done the same thing here. But, with that head injury, he hadn't looked good. He was a big kid, and it would take a lot to keep him down. But he'd been hurting. For that reason alone, she'd expected him to be inside his room. That he hadn't been had completely thrown her.

She showered and changed. When she stepped out of her room again, she still hadn't heard from either one. She sent Dr. Walker and Tony a message, saying she was ready for dinner and was heading down to the lobby. Both responded within a few minutes, saying they were on their way.

On their way maybe, but she didn't see them. Still, that wasn't an issue. It was a big hotel. And Dr. Walker had most likely spent his entire time in the pub. It was one of his favorite occupations, and she could hardly blame him with a situation like this. Everybody had to deal with nerves in their own way, and she was hardly one to criticize.

Still, it helped an awful lot for her to connect with the others. They'd been a fairly close-knit team. Or at least she had thought so. Underneath though, apparently they were just fragmented individuals thrown together for a week. Apparently not even caring about the others.

Saddened by the circumstances that led to all this mistrust, she chose to take the stairs down. At the front desk, she saw the same person she had spoken to earlier about Jasper. She walked over and asked if Jasper had returned.

The man looked at her in surprise and then shook his head. "I haven't seen him. That doesn't mean he didn't come in when I wasn't looking though," he said apologetically.

She smiled at him. "Absolutely. I'm not holding you responsible. I'm just worried about him."

She watched as a tinge of relief crossed his face and realized just how difficult his job was. He had to walk a balancing act between privacy issues and the hotel rules and regulations and what was the right thing to do as a human being for another in trouble.

She patted the top of the desk gently, turned and wandered the very large lobby. All kinds of different seating areas here made it an interesting place to people watch. She could pick up all kinds of different vantage points.

Both men had said they would be here soon, so she didn't want to get too comfortable. She wandered around, looking at the large maps and old photos on the walls. The area had a fascinating history. Pirates had really ruled down here, but a lot of them hadn't bothered coming this far. Only a couple strong men had upheld the tradition. Because there was less competition, the pickings were that much better.

When still nobody showed up a good five minutes later, she frowned and turned to study the people in the lobby. A couple women sat together, having what looked like tea, and a single man who looked to be in his late seventies sat alone, reading a newspaper. Frowning she pulled out her phone and sent a text to Tony. **Where are you?**

And got no answer.

Worried now, she headed toward the elevator. As she hit the button to bring it to her, the double doors opened, and both men stepped out.

She groaned with relief. "There you are," she said. "I'm afraid all of this is getting to me. When you guys didn't show up, I got worried."

Dr. Walker looked at her with that supercilious amusement he always had. "We're totally fine, as you can see." He glanced around as they walked forward. "Now where's Vince and Johan? Our rescuers." His voice held a light arrogant tone. "The men we're supposed to take out for dinner as a thank-you."

"It seems like the least we could do," Vanessa said quietly, stepping up beside them.

Dr. Walker laughed, but Tony took her seriously. "And that's what this is, isn't it? We came very close to not making it."

"Rubbish," Dr. Walker said. "We could have lasted four or five days out there."

"We could have," Tony said. "But that doesn't mean we would have done it in any comfort or that anybody would have found us in that time. An awful lot of empty ocean surrounded us. It's not like we had a search party looking for us."

"But that's exactly what we did have," Dr. Walker said. "Who organized that, by the way? Because really, he's the one we should be thanking."

She glared at him. "My father organized it."

Dr. Walker looked at her in surprise. "Really?"

She nodded. "I've already spoken to him. And it was at his behest that Vince and Johan came after us."

"Oh!"

It was obvious her words had thrown him, as if he thought she didn't have anybody who cared. And that was something she thought pretty odd because he was the one with a family, but had they done anything to go looking for him? Or was it because his wife, being female, sitting at home with young twins, that Dr. Walker hadn't expected her to sound the alarm? Then again he was quite a sexist male, and that was what she would expect from him. But then maybe she was putting that on him. Just because she had a problem with him didn't mean anybody else did.

"Thank him for us, will you?" Tony said. "I, for one, am grateful to have my life."

She smiled up at him. "Indeed. I can send you his email, and you can thank him personally. I don't know how much money this cost, but you can imagine it was in the tens of thousands."

Both men winced.

"Hopefully, he's not asking for a percentage of that back," Dr. Walker snapped. "I certainly don't have that kind of funds to spend."

"Of course, you don't," Tony said. "Nothing is more important than your life, is there?"

They walked straight through to the front doors, still

squabbling. As they stepped outside, the air-conditioning drained away, and the heat hit. Vanessa took several deep breaths, getting used to the humidity and then smiled. She pointed across the street to Vince and Johan walking toward them. "There they are," she cried out.

"Any sign of Jasper?" Tony asked, standing beside her.

She pulled out her phone to see if there was any response. "I don't see him, and I didn't hear from him. And I sure as hell wish he'd check in."

"But he doesn't have to check in, does he?" Dr. Walker said. "He's a grown man. If he's got plans, then he's got plans."

She shoved her phone in her pocket as the men reached her. "He might have plans," she said, and then, just to be an ass, she added, "or somebody else has plans for him."

Both men turned and looked at her.

She shrugged. "We have no clue what's going on with Dr. Sanchez, so there's no way we can assume *anything* when it comes to Jasper."

"I surely hope nothing has befallen him," Tony said. "He's one of the best assistants we've ever had. As a researcher, he's best, bar none."

"Sure," she said. "But he was also Dr. Sanchez's assistant. So, if something has happened to her, what's the chance that, just by association, something has happened to him?"

The two men joined them. Vince looked down at her and smiled. "You look better."

She laughed. "Meaning, I looked like shit before?"

He shook his head. When she raised an eyebrow, he gave a slight shrug. "Let's just say your tough day showed earlier."

"Very nicely put," she said. "I am feeling much better. A shower and a change of clothes will do that. However, none of us have managed to find Jasper."

"And nobody we have talked to has seen him," Vince said, holding up both photos of Dr. Sanchez and Jasper.

She studied them. Something about seeing them in black-and-white photos hit her stomach harshly. "You really think something has happened to them?"

"We know," Johan said, his voice hard, "that something has happened to Dr. Sanchez."

Feeling stupid, she quickly waved her hand. "I know that. I know that. But having Jasper's face right there ... only to not be here all of a sudden, I'm hoping he just went for a walk or is sitting in a restaurant somewhere."

"And he could have gone back to his room. Did either of you check there?" Dr. Walker asked, his snide tone evident.

"He left his phone behind, so we can't text him. And he cannot respond. If he went back to his room," Vanessa said, her frustration rising to match his, "then he would have seen the texts on his phone and answered them."

"Possibly," he conceded. "But we don't know that."

"What we do know is they're both missing," Johan said.

"And under very different circumstances," Tony said. "Surely they're not connected."

"The fact that they're both missing from the same research team," Vince said, "means they are connected. Different circumstances though."

"Jasper isn't missing until it's at least been twenty-four hours, right?"

"Hardly," Vince said. "He could be classed as missing immediately. There's absolutely no way to know what's happened to him." He changed the subject. "We found a nice restaurant around the corner, more outside than in, and appears to be local food, if you're up for that. Otherwise, we can stay here at the hotel."

Vanessa brightened at the thought of a local eatery.

But Dr. Walker spoke his mind. "The hotel will be better."

Her response was a grimace.

Vince grinned at her. "He doesn't get to make that decision," he said. "There's five of us."

She looked over at Tony who half rolled his eyes at her.

"We all prefer eating locally," Tony said. "But Dr. Walker has this thing about not eating food he doesn't recognize. So the hotel food would be much easier on him."

She gave in gracefully because she knew that was true. They had taken him a couple times to dinner at places against his wishes, and he had been violently ill afterward. She'd half wondered if he hadn't shoved his fingers down his throat just to make it happen. She nodded. "That's true. The hotel it is then."

Vince nodded, hooked his arm through hers and said, "Then maybe tomorrow, if we're still here, we'll try a local restaurant for lunch."

She brightened and nodded. "I'm up for it."

"I'd rather be on my way home," Tony said. "I don't understand what the holdup is on getting flights."

"Likely paperwork, either that or for questioning or both," Vanessa said cheerfully. "You know the university has to book all that stuff. We're off schedule, so it's quite possible we'll just stay here because our flights were due to go out tomorrow anyway. It's probably cheaper for them to keep us here in the hotel than it is to change the flights."

Dr. Walker's face looked a shade paler, but he nodded. "Quite possible. But I was really hoping to go home as early as possible."

"How many kids do you have, Dr. Walker?" Vince asked cheerfully.

Dr. Walker smiled. "Twin boys. They're eight now."

"Lovely," Johan said with a grin. "There's nothing like sons, and twins would just double the fun."

"And double the trouble and the expense," Dr. Walker said dourly. But there was a twinkle to his eye.

"Anybody else got kids?" Vince asked the group in general.

Vanessa shook her head. "Nope, not me. Tony, I don't think you do either, do you?"

He shook his head. "Dr. Walker is the only family man among us."

"Neither Jasper nor Dr. Sanchez either?" Johan asked curiously.

Vanessa shook her head. "As far as I know, nope."

The men shrugged and nodded. She figured it was both a question to see just who and what the group was like and also digging a little bit more about Dr. Sanchez.

"I think I'm also the only one who's married," Dr. Walker said, as if that was an achievement in itself.

Then again, considering he'd been married for fourteen years to some poor berated woman, it probably was an achievement. "I'm not," Vanessa said. "Jasper isn't. Tony isn't. Laura might have been at some point, but I don't remember."

The men nodded.

At that point the maître d' asked how many for a table and then asked them to wait and disappeared.

It was a very nice restaurant, so she half expected the high-class treatment, but it seemed a little overdone when most of the customers were in shorts and sandals. But whatever, as long as she got to eat.

As they were seated, drinks were ordered, menus handed out, she settled in against the window, studying the vista outside. She was much more of an outdoors girl and would have been more than happy with a beer and local fare on a side street. But she could also dress up and be a good girl in a nice restaurant too. It wasn't the time to really cause fights. They had enough discord with the now two missing persons from their team.

She looked at the menu and smiled. "At least there are some local favorites on here." She ordered a seafood appetizer and pasta with seafood dish. When she closed the menu, Vince stared at her. "What's the matter?"

"Nothing. Just didn't realize you liked seafood so much."

"I love it, and when I can get it local and fresh …"

He nodded and ordered the exact same thing. She didn't know if he did it on purpose or because he really wanted it.

With the other orders in, an uncomfortable silence settled on the table. She looked for a conversation starter and then said brightly, "I know you were hired by my dad, but, as part of the group you rescued, I really appreciate you coming and saving our sorry asses. So, thank you."

Both men looked at her in surprise but nodded their heads.

"You're welcome," Vince said. "And you're right. Your father did arrange this. But the university would have also. We've been in contact with them steadily, now that we've arrived and found you. And they're quite concerned about Dr. Sanchez."

"But what can we do about it now?" Tony asked, puzzled. "Surely the local authorities are looking for her."

"They are, indeed," Vince said. "But that doesn't mean they will have any luck. It would help a lot to know where her last movements were. And, of course, we wanted Jasper for that."

VINCE HAD BEEN keeping track of the people coming and going in the restaurant, just to see if he didn't like something going on here. He was still working out where Jasper was. It didn't feel right. But, with nobody talking and nobody having seen any sign of him, it was like Jasper had dropped off the edge of the earth. Kind of like Dr. Sanchez.

Vince waited as the waitress returned, her arms laden with their meals. He checked his phone several times while she delivered their meals.

Vanessa leaned across the table. "What are you expecting?"

He shrugged and said, "Anything at this point. I'd really like to see one of those two people show up."

"You know she won't show up again," Dr. Walker said. "I hate to be the bearer of bad news, but let's get real. She's probably lost at sea."

"I don't think so," Johan said calmly. "I think she was either taken off the ship by force, or she left on her own. There's such a major gap between the time anybody last saw her and when you were taken prisoner that anything could have happened."

"But why?" Vanessa asked.

Vince watched as she picked up a huge succulent shrimp and bit into half of it. The pleasure that wafted across her face gave an instant physical reaction. This was a woman who would be passionate no matter what she did. She would eat well; she would play well, and life would give her all kinds of good things because she was someone who took the time to enjoy the small things. And, when she got something extra-special, she would make sure she enjoyed it. He had to admire that.

He looked down at his own plate, heaped high with prawns and grinned. He picked up the first one and popped the whole thing into his mouth. And even he had to stop and close his eyes. Fresh lemon squirted into his mouth along with the wonderful flavors of fresh seafood. There was seafood, and then there was *this* seafood. He swore to God they must have been picked out of the sea within the last hour because it was so fresh tasting.

"Aren't they good?" Vanessa asked in amazement. "I can't believe how fresh they are."

Vince nodded and didn't waste time on words. Only the two of them had ordered seafood, and he was fine with that.

Dr. Walker had stuck with tried-and-true steak and a baked potato. Vince figured Walker probably ordered that no matter where he was. Not everybody's comfort level extended to trying new and different things in other parts of world. As Vince looked at his plate, he realized his wasn't all that unusual. It was fresh seafood with pasta. That was pretty standard no matter where you were. It was just the quality of the actual food that made his stomach sing with joy.

Another waitress refilled their water glasses. He looked up at her and smiled. "You must get a lot of tourists through here," he said.

"Tourists, researchers, lots of workmen," she said with a grin. She looked at the people at this table, and her eyes narrowed. "Aren't you part of the research team from the university with Dr. Sanchez?"

Silence fell on the table.

Vince said encouragingly, "Yes. Have you seen Dr. Sanchez lately?"

The waitress shook her head and smiled. "No, I haven't. But I did see Jasper this morning."

"Oh, interesting," he said lightly. "Where did you see him? We were trying to contact him to invite him to dinner."

The woman looked surprised. She checked her watch and said, "It was probably a good six or seven hours ago. He was walking out of the hotel."

"Darn," Vince said. "We were hoping he was around."

"I don't think so," she said with a frown. "And he wasn't alone. Two men in black suits were with him." She glanced at the others and said, "That's one of the reasons why I came over here. I was hoping you'd seen him since. There was just something about the way the men were talking to him that was a little unnerving. But I was coming on my shift and was late already. So I didn't give it too much thought. Until I saw you guys, and I remembered how unnerved Jasper looked."

"You know Jasper well, do you?" Vince asked.

She flushed.

He realized his intuition had hit that one on the head.

"Well enough," she said hurriedly. "He's a really nice man."

Vanessa smiled up at her. "He's a wonderful man. Would you recognize the two men he was with? Did they get in a vehicle and drive away, or did they walk?"

"They got into a vehicle. I think it was a black car," she said with a frown. "But again, I'm sorry. I just caught him in a glance, recognized he wasn't very happy and came inside."

"Did he see you?"

The waitress nodded. "Yes. He flashed me a bright smile. I guess that's why I wasn't thinking anything was wrong."

"So you didn't actually see him get into the vehicle?" Johan asked.

She frowned and looked down at him. "Not really. I did see him stand at the back, and one of the men was waiting for him to get in. They were kind of blocking his exit so he couldn't back out. No, no," she said hurriedly, "I don't know. I can't really say what it was about it that bothered me." And then she caught sight of someone on the other side of the restaurant. "I have to go." She hurried away.

"Interesting," Dr. Walker said. "I didn't think Jasper knew anyone here."

"Apparently he does," Johan said with a nod at the waitress.

Dr. Walker grinned. "Jasper is a healthy young man, but, as for those two men in black, I don't know." He frowned. "Government men?"

"That's an interesting guess," Vince said, pulling out his phone. He sent Levi a text with an update. "It'd be easy enough to check."

"Not really," Dr. Walker said. "The government around here is notoriously unstable. You'll get a yes one day and a no the next day."

"I think that's standard for governments all over the world," Johan said. "Doesn't really matter which one it is."

Vanessa chuckled. "Isn't that the truth. It goes for all microcities too, like a university system. Just when you think you got your grants and all your paperwork in order, they turn around and say, *Nope, you don't. You're missing something, and until you do it, you can't have whatever it is you are after."*

"And maybe that's standard for all companies," Vince said. "Besides, a quick check at the government level here will see if he's their guest," Johan said lightly. "A consulate is here as well. Maybe he's there."

"Oh, now that's a great idea," Tony said. "I never even thought of that."

With several more emails fired off, Vince returned to his meal. When his texts came in several at a time, the others all watched as he calmly ate his shrimp. He looked up and grinned. "They can wait thirty seconds. This is an excellent meal, and I intend to enjoy it."

But, after a couple more bites, he pulled out his phone and flicked through Levi's responses.

He said in a noncommittal voice, "Levi is following up on it. There are very little security or traffic cams here, but he's checking with the government and the embassy."

"That's good to know," she said. "Maybe somebody can roust out some answers."

Just then her phone dinged. She pulled it up and said with delighted surprise, "It's from Jasper."

She flicked her screen to bring up the message. All the color drained from her face. She stared up at them. "He says he's in trouble, and he needs help."

"What kind of help?" Johan asked.

"He doesn't say." Her fingers were busy texting him back. **Absolutely. Where are you? What can we do?** She hit Send. "What kind of trouble could he be in?"

"It's hard to say," Johan said. "At least he's alive. That is a really good solid step."

Vince nodded grimly. "But for how long?"

Chapter 10

"**A**T LEAST HE'S alive. I guess that means he did come back to his room and grabbed his phone. He had to have seen all of our messages though," she repeated out loud. "God, is this what our world has come to?"

"Considering Dr. Sanchez is missing," Vince said, "and Jasper disappeared without any word to any of us, yes."

"Why wouldn't he have texted me earlier?" she said, looking down at her phone, waiting to see if she would get a response.

"Because he couldn't," Tony said. "It's the only answer that makes any sense."

She looked over at him, hearing the quake in his voice. Tony was one of the best scientists she knew, but he wasn't into this cloak-and-dagger stuff and definitely not into a dangerous lifestyle. He loved his rocking chair, his pipe and a fireplace. He had two beagles at home, waiting for him. And she understood the kind of guy he was. He was very similar to her father in many ways. Just thirty years younger.

She laid the phone on the table as she continued to eat, her gaze constantly on her phone, waiting to see if something came in. When there was nothing, she looked up at Vince.

He smiled at her reassuringly. "Depending on the kind of trouble, you know we have help available."

She swallowed hard and took another bite. "I just don't

understand what kind of trouble."

"No," he said, "but just the fact that there *is* trouble might be enough to get some help. My boss will contact the consulate and see if they know anything about it."

"What about the people who give us the permits? Maybe they can find out if there's been any kind of trouble with the research team."

At that moment, taking the last bite from his plate, Vince looked up and saw four men outside the double glass entrance to the main lobby of the hotel, all similarly dressed in some uniform. ... Law enforcement maybe? Or military? They crossed the entrance and headed toward the front reception desk. Vince glanced at Johan and saw his gaze had narrowed, his face frozen, and said, "Trouble just arrived, don't you think? Or are they on our side? Or does their presence have nothing to do with us?"

"I'm thinking *trouble*. And for *us*. There's nothing amiable about their looks. I'd rather be safe than sorry." Johan glanced around. "We better find a back exit for our friends here."

Not giving them a chance to argue, Vince moved all three into Johan's care, moving them out the restaurant through the kitchen. He wasn't even sure where that would take them. He walked over to the front counter and paid the bill, then casually walked out to the lobby.

Vanessa had followed behind him.

He turned and glared at her. "Those men are coming for you," he snapped in a low tone. "Don't you get that?"

She glared back. "I saw you send the others away, but it's no good if you'll be left behind. I watched you pay the bill and then head out to the front."

"I was trying to see where the men were going," he said.

"Whether reception sends them up to our rooms or over to the restaurant. I needed to know what window of time we had, which now you have just narrowed considerably."

Ouch. She hadn't meant to cause any trouble, but she hadn't wanted him to get in trouble either. "You can't be the one taken," she hissed. "You're the only one who knows how to get us out of here."

"Which is why we split up," he said, urging her through the restaurant to the back. "Johan is just as good as I am. But we can't do anything if you guys get picked up."

"Sure you can," she said. "You rescued us once. You can rescue us again."

"I could," he said, "but it'll be an entirely different story this time. It's not pirates. It's local law enforcement."

"I think they were militia," she muttered. Before she realized it, she stood outside in the setting sun. She looked around, but there was no sign of Johan and the others. "We're separated from them, aren't we?"

"Of course you are," he said. "Remember that part about going with him?"

She nodded but stayed silent. This was her fault. But she'd done it for the best of reasons. She'd already lost Laura; she wouldn't lose Vince too.

VINCE WAS MORE than pissed that she hadn't followed his orders, and that now stopped him from having a chance to see what was going on in the lobby. He grabbed her arm and tugged her around the block. "Stay at my side," he said in a harsh whisper. "Don't try to look like you're running. Just stay beside me as if we have a place to go and a time frame to be there."

"I wouldn't have to run," she said, gasping, "if you would slow down."

He slowed his pace. "We can't slow too much," he warned. "We have to meet up with the others."

Biting her lip, she stayed at his side.

He damn-well hoped so. After what she'd cost him in time back at the restaurant, it would be hard to figure out what was going on now. He saw no sign of the four men. He didn't have an informant inside the hotel. And that was too damn bad. He also didn't want to think they'd lost or forfeited the contents of their rooms. His laptop was there, as were his traveling papers.

He thought about how he could get back into the hotel and grab everybody's gear without being seen. Up ahead he saw Johan waiting for them on a small park bench. They met up, and, in a low voice, Vince said to Johan, "I didn't get a chance to see where they went. My concern is they went up to our rooms."

Johann nodded grimly. "Take them. I'll collect our stuff."

"You can't go alone," Vanessa argued. "It's too much stuff."

He gave her a hard look. "It means you won't get it all back." And, just like that, he disappeared.

The two men looked at him. "What's going on?" Dr. Walker asked.

"Those men were looking for you," Vince said. "We're trying to delay that from happening."

"Delay?" Tony asked. "But you're expecting them to get us eventually?"

He shook his head. "I hope not. Who are they? What do they want?"

"If they're government," Dr. Walker said, "maybe we should see them. They can't be on the wrong side of this. They're probably just looking for more information on Dr. Sanchez."

"Yes, they quite possibly are," Vince said with a heavy sigh. "Think about it. There were five of you on the boat. Four came back. And none of you have anything to say about the missing doctor. Yet, she has friends in high places, people who want her, and maybe not for the right reasons. Can't you see how the government might be willing to look sideways for answers?"

Dr. Walker frowned at Vince, and he could see Dr. Walker didn't get it. "They'll be quite happy to charge you guys with her murder," he said abruptly. "Or at least say you're responsible for her going missing."

"We didn't have anything to do with it," Tony protested.

"But they won't care, will they?" Vanessa asked, staring up at Vince. "Jesus, what have we gotten into?"

"So why the hell couldn't we have left today?" Dr. Walker jumped to his feet and paced in a circle. "If we'd managed to get on flights, it would have been a done deal." He lightly smacked Vanessa on the shoulder. "You probably told them it was cheaper to keep us here because you were trying to get Dr. Sanchez," he said contemptuously.

She glared at him. "Yes, I am concerned about Laura. But I didn't have anything to do with the university making that call. Our flights are booked for tomorrow. Whether the local military or the local government know about that is a different story. If we can get checked through on the airlines, we could still leave on time."

Vince kept his thoughts to himself, but, if the government wanted to nab them, it was pretty easy to check for flights for these four. What he didn't know was what role Jasper had in all of this.

"Has anybody heard from Jasper since that first text?"

They all pulled out their phones. One at a time they each shook their heads. Vince stared off in the distance. "The last thing I want to do is have you guys picked up by these men."

"Why is that?" Dr. Walker asked. "It's not like they can turn around and slam us into jail and ignore us. We're American citizens, for God's sake."

"That doesn't mean we're God," Tony said, turning on him suddenly. "And they don't give a shit what country we come from. Here, we're in their country. Can you at least try to remember you're not somebody special here?"

Dr. Walker glared at him, but he settled back on the bench. "I'm never getting home, am I?"

"I'm more concerned about Dr. Sanchez and Jasper at this moment," Vanessa said suddenly. "There's got to be a way to get through to Jasper."

"Maybe, but if he's not answering his phone and if no one has seen him ..."

"We need to see if he's been kidnapped," she said in a rush. "Maybe we can contact his captors. Find a way to rescue Jasper."

"Yeah, and get taken by the same men." Tony raised both hands in frustration. "That won't work because, if we are taken by the same group, we might not be placed in the same room the next time." He sat down beside Dr. Walker and looked up at Vince. "This is your area of specialty. What the hell are we supposed to do now?"

Vince worked out a plan. "We'll find a place to hide.

And then we'll send out feelers to see what the hell's going on, which group is looking for you guys."

"And where is it we could possibly hide?" Dr. Walker sneered. "They already know we're registered at the hotel, so they'll be watching for us there."

"Yes. So we won't be there." He looked around the neighborhood, wondering about the best location. He pulled out his phone and sent a text to Levi, saying he needed housing for five because an unknown group had come to the hotel looking for them.

"Do you think there's any chance it wasn't us they were looking for?" Tony asked hesitantly. "I know we all jumped to the same conclusion after hearing about Jasper, but do we really know for sure they came after us?"

Dr. Walker pulled out his phone. "One way to find out." He hit a series of numbers on his phone while Vince watched him.

"Who are you calling?" Vanessa asked.

He held up a finger to silence her. "Yes. Hello. This is Dr. Walker. I registered earlier today. I was just wondering if there are any messages at the front desk for me." He winced at whatever the other person said. "Oh, interesting. Well, I certainly don't know what the problem is. I'll be sure to contact them. Yes, yes, I'll be back very quickly." He hung up and turned to Vince. "They said law enforcement was looking for us. They had some questions they wanted us to answer."

Vince snagged his phone, popped open the back and pulled out the SIM card and the battery. Then he handed him his phone and pocketed both items.

Dr. Walker looked at him in horror. "What did you just do?"

"I stopped them from tracking your damn phone."

Dr. Walker stared at him. "How could they possibly do that? They don't have my number." Then he realized what he'd said and who he'd just called and sighed. "So what you're saying is that they know I'm alive and have a phone with me. They can track that back."

"Certainly law enforcement could. I know I certainly could," Vince said. He looked at the other two and flicked out his hands. "Same for you guys."

"What about you?" Tony asked as he handed him the battery and SIM card from his phone.

"I have two phones," Vince said. "Neither of them are on, and neither of them are registered at the hotel."

"Why is that?"

"For exactly the same reason we're taking yours away from you."

Dejected, the three sat on the bench, while Vince checked for messages on his own phone. Levi came through with a name and an address. He brought it up on his GPS, noted where they were and how far away they were and nodded. "Come on. Let's go."

Ushering the group ahead of him, he sent a text to Johan about their future location but in code, in case he was taken and somebody found his phone. Vince maneuvered the group down several blocks, over one and up another. By the time they arrived at the destination, they were hot, sweaty and protesting loudly.

He groaned as they entered the cool reception room and smiled at the lady who met them in the entranceway. She chattered away and handed him two room keys. He nodded and led them straight through.

Upstairs he opened two rooms and put the men in together, keeping Vanessa with him. When they went in the other side, he walked through and opened the adjoining room.

"Why won't she tell the police?" Tony asked as he walked through to their room.

"She would if she had any idea the police were looking for us," Vince said cheerfully. "But since she's hiding from the police herself, she's not likely to check."

"How did you find that out?" Vanessa asked.

He shot her a slanted look and stayed quiet. Then he said, "Double beds are here. And nobody is to leave these rooms."

"Until when?"

"Until Johan gets here," he said. "That will determine whether we'll have the paperwork and documentation necessary for you to leave the country."

That shut them all up.

"If they're watching for us at the airport, how will we get out of here?" Vanessa asked.

"That sailboat we used to rescue you may end up taking us out of here," he said, "but I don't have that locked down yet."

Vanessa walked over to the first bed and sat down near the headboard. "Good thing we just ate then. I should be fine for a couple hours."

He appreciated the steadfastness of her manner.

Tony sat down on the other bed. "Instead of getting us out of a pickle, it seems like we're getting further and further into one, and none of this explains where Jasper or Dr. Sanchez are."

"All we can do is circle around here," Vanessa said. "We're not getting any answers."

"My team has sent out lots of feelers," Vince said. "We lay low until some of those feelers bear fruit, and we get some answers. There's no point in running around lost and getting ourselves into more trouble."

His phone buzzed. He pulled it out to see a message from Johan. "Johan is on his way back."

"Did he get our passports?" Dr. Walker asked. "If he didn't, then I feel like I should go to the authorities, speak with them myself, and then go back to my hotel and get a decent night's sleep, so I can fly out tomorrow."

Vanessa shook her head. "Don't do that, Dr. Walker. You know that's not the right thing to do."

He gave her an astonished look. "My dear, it's law enforcement. They're not executioners. I know we're not on American soil, but they do understand the kind of trouble they'll have if they treat us poorly."

Vince snorted and stared at him in wonder. He didn't know if Walker actually believed what he was saying or if he was just trying to say something to make himself feel better. Either way it was all blarney. But Vince could understand from his point of view that maybe he was grabbing at straws to get out of this mess. He knew in his heart of hearts it wouldn't work. But he wouldn't force the man to stay.

"You do what you think is best," Vince said. "My advice is to stay here and to avoid problems. But, if you want to turn yourself in, then do so. And good luck."

Dr. Walker stared at him and slowly said, "Maybe I will."

Vanessa jumped to her feet. "Please don't."

He brushed away her concerns. "You're worrying too much. All this cloak-and-dagger stuff, it's turning your brain into thinking we're in some Bond movie." And then he walked out of the room.

Tony and Vanessa looked at each other and then at Vince. "Why did you tell him that?"

"Because it's true," Vince said. "I won't sit here and argue with somebody who doesn't want to be saved. I'll have enough trouble keeping you guys safe. I don't need somebody who doesn't want to be looked after. That's just the way of it."

She sagged back on the bed.

Vince had pulled out his phone again.

"You know he'll tell them where we are, don't you?" Tony said. "Dr. Walker is one thing and one thing only, and that is concerned about his own ass."

Vince sighed. "Yes, I do know." He made a call.

Chapter 11

S HE WAS STUNNED to hear him speak a variation of Spanish. And he did it well. When he was done and hung up the phone, she looked at him and said, "Now what did you just do?"

"I changed our rooms. They have a sister hotel around the corner. It's more low-key. You'll love it." He nudged them both up. "Come on. Let's go. No time like the present."

"Don't you think we should wait a little bit," she said. "In case Dr. Walker changes his mind."

Vince looked out the window. As he watched, Dr. Walker stepped across the road and headed down to the main street. Vince kept watching for several minutes until two vehicles pulled up on either side of Dr. Walker. Vince closed the curtains. "Go, now." He grabbed their hands and ran them from their hotel room to the back stairs and outside.

"What's the rush?" she asked, racing beside him.

"Dr. Walker was just picked up."

Outside he immersed the three of them in the crowds, then texted Johan with a new address. He didn't get confirmation and didn't waste his time waiting for it either. Keeping to the back alleys he moved them through to the next lodging. Going in the back door, he made his way up the back stairs.

A young boy stood beside a door. He had a big grin on his face and a key in his hand. Vince took the key, handed him a few coins, opened the door and moved everybody inside. Then the door closed. Inside were two large double beds. Tony sighed. "I'll get sick of double beds very quickly."

"It seems like our lodgings are getting smaller and smaller," Vanessa said with a poor attempt at a laugh. She sagged on the nearest bed and looked up at Vince. "You think it's bad news he was picked up, don't you?"

Tony looked at her. "Even *I* think it's bad news he was picked up so fast. It means they were already looking for us."

"Of course they were," she said. "They want to talk to us and to ask questions. How long do we wait here?"

"Until I can get more answers." Vince looked around the small room and walked into the bathroom. After using the facilities, he came out with a drink of water in his hand. "And we wait for Johan. That will tell us what we have available to work with." He studied the two people in front of him. "It'll work out. I promise."

Vanessa gave him a wan smile. "It's not that I don't believe you because, if there's anybody who can make this happen or make this all go away, it's you. We never expected to survive the ocean."

"How did you get our coordinates for that anyway?" Tony asked.

"We were going off the last GPS coordinates for the research vessel," Vince said. "We were prepared to be out there for a week if need be."

Tony sighed. "I don't trust Dr. Walker," he said suddenly. "I really don't trust him to not turn us in."

"I'm pretty sure they've already gone to our first hotel

rooms," Vince said. "The thing is, we don't know if they can find us here too."

"Will the first hotel tell them?"

He shook his head. "No. This is the lawless land. Nobody'll tell on us."

"Except for more money," she said. "It's a very poor area of town."

"True." He flashed her a grin. "But they've already been paid, and they'll get paid more if we're left alone. And everybody wants that second payment."

She nodded. "I guess we can't have any contact with anybody either, can we?"

"No," he said. "Not right now. Complete blackout."

"My father will worry."

"Your father has already contacted the consulate, looking for you," Vince said. "My boss put him onto that as soon as they realized we were in trouble."

"Why would that make a difference?" Tony asked.

"To make waves to ensure you don't just disappear off the face of the earth."

That shut them up. Vanessa sat back on the bed. "I'm tired."

"Nap," he urged. "Just close your eyes and let all this float away. I'll wake you if I need to move us real fast."

Tony nodded. "Me too," he said. "Because it's cramped quarters, I'll lie down beside her. But if anything happens, you promise you'll wake us?"

"I promise."

ABOUT FORTY-FIVE MINUTES later a faint knock came at the door. Vince slipped up to it and peeked through the peephole. It was Johan. He unlocked the door and let him in. With the door closing behind him, he rebolted it and turned to him. "Well?"

"It's FUBAR," Johan said with a grin. "Makes life exciting." He dropped the several backpacks he carried. Vince looked at him. "Documents?"

"Passports, documents, purse, wallets, laptops, etcetera."

"But not the bags?"

"Too many bags for me to carry. After getting your text, I left Dr. Walker's alone."

"All of it?"

Johan shrugged. "No. I have his passport and wallet. But I didn't take anything else from his room."

"Good, then at least if we can find him, we can still get him out of the country."

"But he's not our problem, is he?"

"No," Vince said, running his hand through hair. "He isn't, but yet, he is."

Johan nodded in agreement. "Never fun when you get somebody with a mind of his own, who doesn't want to listen to the experts."

"Exactly," Vince said. He motioned to Vanessa and Tony, napping quietly. "We need a plan."

"We need information," Johan corrected. "The streets are buzzing. They're looking for four of us. That means we can't travel together anymore."

"Agreed," Vince said. "I was thinking we should take the sailboat and head out of the country that way."

"The airport will definitely be watched," Johan said, "though that's the easiest and fastest way home. But that's only if they can make the flights, and the flights don't get canceled. And the team isn't stopped before boarding."

"We don't have time to buy fake IDs and get them out that way either," Vince said.

"We'll wait on the information as it comes in. I'm more concerned about what Dr. Walker will be telling them than anything else."

Vince winced. "According to these two, he's likely to spill his guts entirely in order to save his own skin."

"It wouldn't be so bad if we had some information about Jasper and Dr. Sanchez," he said. "But chances are, all Walker will do is turn us in."

Chapter 12

VANESSA WOKE UP slowly. She could hear Vince and Johan talking behind her. In front of her Tony lay slumbering gently. Memories came flooding back. They were on the run, apparently from law enforcement and potentially pirates. None of this made any sense, and all she wanted to do, she realized, was to echo Dr. Walker's refrain to go home.

She wondered just what the scenario was with Dr. Walker, but, with all their phones now out of commission, it was hard just to get a reading on the situation. She desperately wanted Vince to say, *Hey, it's all good. Come answer a few questions for the locals, and then we can hit our flights tomorrow.* But she knew that would not happen.

"Any news?" she murmured.

"Some," Vince said, walking around to her side of the bed.

She rolled over so she faced Vince and Johan. They sat in two chairs facing each other. She had no idea how the chairs arrived. Knowing them, they probably took them from another room. "What's up?"

"Levi has talked to the consulate. They have no word of any law enforcement holding Jasper."

Vanessa's gut twisted. "And do they have any idea about Dr. Walker?"

"No," Johan answered. "We just heard from them five minutes ago. Nobody has seen either of them."

"So who were the men who picked up Dr. Walker?"

"That's anybody's guess. The consulate said they've been having trouble with various gangs. But he couldn't see how that was connected to your case."

"No, it'll be connected to Laura," she said sadly. "We just don't know in what way."

"I think you're right," Vince said. "What we need to do is lie low."

"Is that the advice you got from the others?" she asked, wishing she could do something—an actionable step instead of this *hanging around, doing nothing* stuff. She'd take action any day. "Just lie low?"

"Yep, pretty much," Vince said. "Remember that part about waiting until we get some information so we actually have something viable to act upon?"

Vanessa pinched the bridge of her nose. "Can Levi contact my father and tell him that I'm okay?"

"Already done." Vince's voice was gentle. "Your father understands what's going on. He's waiting for any updates, the same as we are."

A heavy sigh released from her chest. She crossed her arms and pulled her knees up tighter. Chilled inside and out, it was hard to imagine how this would work out. "Does anybody have any word on Laura?"

"Nothing yet," Vince said. "We have informants in Colombia. Everybody is looking for her."

"But, if she was kidnapped and smuggled into the country, nobody will have seen her, will they?"

"Now there's a possibility," Vince said. "In that case, we don't have any way to know for sure what's going on."

She sat up and glared at them. "So what is it you do know?"

Vince grinned at her.

She glared deeper.

"I know we need to stay low, to stay out of sight and to stay out of trouble."

"So why don't we just get back on that sailboat of yours and head down the coast?" she asked. "Or up the coast. I really don't care which country we go to."

"It's possible," Johan said. "We've been cleared to do that. But are you sure you want to do it without Jasper and Dr. Walker and Dr. Sanchez?"

She felt like a shit. "No," she muttered. "God, no. It's bad enough we don't have Laura with us, but now with those two missing also, this is just getting worse and worse. I don't have a clue how to find even those two men."

"No," Vince said, "neither do we. And, of course, time is on our side, given that they're probably safe somewhere. But that doesn't mean Dr. Sanchez is safe."

Just then Vince's phone went off again. It was a weird buzzing sound. But instead of checking the text, he lifted it to his ear. "Yes?" he answered. Obviously he knew who it was. He looked to Vanessa and nodded. "We can take them to a safe place, yes, but they won't want to leave without the other two members of their team. Of Dr. Sanchez, we have no clue."

They talked some more, but none of it gave her any answers. When he finally hung up, he said, "We're moving to the sailboat tonight. We'll go out into international waters and stay there until we get more answers."

She looked at him, her stomach twisting yet again. "And Dr. Walker and Jasper?"

"If we have you safe on board the boat, we can then go after those two."

"Go after?" she said on a bitter laugh. "We don't even know where they are. How can you go after anyone?"

"We did get the license plate," Johan volunteered reluctantly. "We're tracking it down now."

"From the vehicle that picked up Dr. Walker?" Tony sat up beside them.

Vince nodded. "We didn't tell you because we didn't know if we could run it down. But, as soon as we have a name, potentially an address, we'll go in search of them."

"And hopefully find both of them?"

Both men nodded.

"Then leave us here," she said. "You will go and get those two. Then all of us can move together."

Vince shook his head. "It's much easier to travel as four than as six. If we get you safely on board the boat, then we'll come back to shore and get the other men."

"Getting us on the sailboat is one thing," she said. "I'd be more than happy to go there. But I don't want you to take us out to international waters. Both Tony and I can run the boat. But, if we're moored somewhere close by for now, we can pull out of the bay on your word if it gets ugly."

Johan studied her face carefully. "What benefit is there to that?"

"It's easier for you guys to get to shore and for you to bring Dr. Walker and Jasper back to the boat."

Vince nodded. "It would be, but it would put you in more danger."

"Does anybody know about your sailboat?" Vanessa asked. "Will anybody suspect we're on it? Because otherwise, I highly suggest we stick to that plan so it's easier for you guys to come back and forth."

The two men studied each other and then shrugged.

"That's a possibility," Johan said. "But what we can't do is make that decision until we know about the black vehicle." It wasn't long until they got another message. Johan's phone lit up. "They've tracked down the owner of the vehicle. And look at that. It is a Colombian national."

"See?" she said excitedly. "It's all got to be related to Laura."

Vince and Johan nodded.

"For the first time we might actually agree with you," Vince said, "now that we have something that connects this. We have an address." He glanced at Tony. "Are you okay to go out to the sailboat?"

Tony nodded. "We're probably safer there where we have a chance of getting away than being sitting ducks here."

"You're pretty safe here," Johan said.

Tony shook his head. "As soon as you pay somebody, there's always somebody who'll pay more. I barely slept, but now that I have, all I feel is this instinct to run."

"Good enough for me," Johan said. He picked up the bags and tossed one to Tony. "That's yours, Jasper's and Dr. Walker's personal documents, passports, wallets, laptops." Another bag Johan threw over his shoulder.

Tony looked down at the collection. "How did you get into the rooms and get all this?"

Johan gave him a bland look.

Tony shrugged, a smile on his face. "Well, the clothes and bags we can replace but this stuff? ... Yes, thank you for that." He quickly checked through it and then zipped it up and put it on his back.

Vanessa went into the bathroom, washed her face, used

the facilities, and, by the time she came out, Vince held her bag. It was her regular backpack she used when she went on day trips. She grabbed it thankfully and checked inside. Indeed, her laptop, wallet, passport and a lot of her research papers were there.

Vince motioned at the outside pocket. "Johan wasn't sure what you might need. But there was a bag full of USB keys."

She looked at him in delight as she dug through the pocket. "Did you bring that?" And there it was. She pulled out the small bag and turned to Tony. "This is all our research."

Tony shook his head. "I forgot we were even about to lose all that. I know we had some on laptops and some in cloud storage, but that, … that's our backup."

"It's likely to be everything," Vanessa said, "because chances are good there won't be a backup on cloud storage, and who knows what's actually been transferred. You know how spotty any communication was."

He nodded.

She shoved the USB keys deep into her pocket. "Thank you, Johan." When she saw her wallet, she pulled it out and found the money was still there and her credit cards. She could feel something good settling inside. She didn't like being without her documentation and money. But now that she had both, she was good to go. She hopped up, and, like Tony, threw it on her back. "Let's go," she said. "I'd rather be on the ship than here."

IT WAS DARK enough and silent enough that it was safe to leave. Sort of. Going out the back exit into the alleyway,

Vince hung on tight to Vanessa. She was just unpredictable enough that he didn't want her going off in a different direction than he was going. He whispered in her ear, "For all intents and purposes you belong to me while we're here. Do you understand?"

She shot him a look but nodded.

He was grateful for that. Vanessa was small, slight, pretty, and she would be valuable goods on the streets. The last thing they needed was to have any kind of argument with a local as to who "owned" Vanessa. And neither did he want to have to slap her around and make a show of dominance for others to see he would protect his property. But, in this part of town, you could damn well be sure that she was nothing but chattel.

With a hard look at Johan and Tony, he led the way. They walked steadily through the back streets. He had the route in his head that would take them to where they needed to go. They passed several groups, but nobody seemed to want to challenge them. Then again, he had also had several staring contests with men as he walked past.

It was a dangerous mission, but, at the same time, it was necessary. Necessary to get them to safety. Because Tony was right. As soon as you paid somebody to do something, always somebody else would be willing to pay more. There was only so much Vince and Johan could do. Vince could protect Vanessa and Tony to a certain extent, but that was it. At some point, all hell would break loose, and he wanted them well out in the middle of the bay before then.

As they came to the large docks, Vince pushed her gently toward Johan. "Stay here," he said in a guttural whisper.

He stepped out into the darkness, surveying the path to the marina. The entrance was locked. He frowned. He hadn't expected that. But then there had to be some kind of security here.

A small rowboat supposedly waiting for them at the end. Not exactly his choice, but any motor would make too much noise. They wanted to be quiet, didn't want to make it look like they were skulking. The trouble was, a rowboat would do the same thing.

He picked the lock on the marina gate and slid down to the docks. As he came to the end, instead of a rowboat there was a canoe. He studied the size of it and nodded. That would work fine. It would allow both Johan and him to put some muscle into the job.

He headed back, rejoined the rest. Moving silently now toward the water, hating the shadows that moved with him when he walked them to the marina, he stopped.

As they gathered, Vanessa whispered, "Did you see anyone?"

Johan looked to Vince. He just shot him a look and slyly pointed to the back wall. Johan disappeared.

Tony asked Vince, "Where's he going?"

Vanessa turned to him. "*Shh.*"

Tony glared at her but then seemed to realize Johan was going after someone. He frowned and followed her into the canoe. He kept glancing back as if to ensure Johan was coming. At one point he turned to Vince and said, "Should he be alone?"

Vince nodded. "Sometimes it's the only way we can do this." He untied the canoe, then got in. Johan would have a ten-minute window, and that was it. Otherwise, Vince would go after him when he got Vanessa and Tony to the boat. He checked his watch and then pushed off but Vanessa and Tony whispered, "Wait. Wait. We can't go without

Johan."

In as quiet a voice as he could manage, because their voices carried over water like loudspeakers, he said, "Remember? I'm going back to the shore."

They fell silent but were obviously not happy about the circumstances. Tony did settle himself to the other end of the canoe, picked up a paddle, and, with Vanessa in the middle, the two men steadily struck their way out to the bay.

"Why didn't you bring the boat in and moor it?"

"Paperwork," he said. He could feel her puzzlement until Tony spoke.

"Moorage fees, registrations, things like that."

She sighed. "It really is a shallow world when you have to think about that."

Vince nodded. When he heard voices from a nearby party boat, he held up his hand with a finger in the air to be quiet.

Stroking strong and silently, they slipped past the party boat and kept going. He could feel the tense atmosphere behind them. He understood it. For him, it was something that drove him. It gave him a certain amount of comfort to realize they'd made it this far. A battle on the water was a battle he was in command of. But he had two innocents, and that gave him a handicap.

It took a little longer than he'd expected. Tony was good, but he wasn't Johan. Eight minutes off his timing, he pulled the canoe up to the side of the sailboat. There he threw up a rope onto the ladder. Secured, he pivoted to help Vanessa climb the ladder. Then, with Tony following, he scooted up behind her. He did a quick search of the boat, found it all good to go, made sure there was gas and that the engines worked, shut her down and whispered, "I'm gone."

"How will we know if there's a problem?" Vanessa asked. She grabbed his hands. "What if something happens to you?"

He knew that partly she was asking because of her own fear and fear of what would happen to them. He handed her one of his two cell phones. "If you get three separate calls in a row, and nobody is there, you turn this boat on and head straight out for international waters, then go up the coast. Understand?"

Both nodded dumbly.

He smiled. "And, of course, if you get a text or phone call, make sure you answer it because I could be on the other end. I'll let you know as soon as I can what we're doing."

She nodded, then kissed him gently on his cheek. "Thank you."

He flashed a wicked grin at her. "Is that the way to send a warrior into battle?" He cupped her face with his hands and kissed her hard and deep and passionately. When he released her, she sagged back against Tony. Vince climbed over the side of the boat, landing easily into the canoe, picked up his paddle, disconnected the rope, and he headed back toward shore.

Chapter 13

"**H**OLY SHIT," TONY said. "You know what? As far as exits go, that was movie-worthy."

His grin was a mile wide, but she could hardly argue with him. "It sure was," she said with a sigh. "And he's a hell of a kisser too."

Tony just chuckled. "Not my style, as you well know."

She grinned. "Well, it would be if he were kissing you," she teased.

He shook his head. "You know who I have at home," he said, "and thanks for not making an issue of it."

She shrugged. "I have absolutely no problem with you having somebody you love and care for at home. I'm just sorry you're not there with him."

Tony nodded. "So am I. It's very painful to be here in this situation and to not know what the hell happened to everyone, to not know if we will ever make it back home again."

She nodded. "But we have to trust in the men. They've done well by us so far."

"I can't imagine the world they live in where they know how to do all this," Tony said. "How they can procure the stuff they need to procure."

"Speaking of which," Vanessa said, "I don't know about you, but I'm hoping at least we can drink something on board." She headed toward the kitchen. "A pot of coffee would not go amiss."

"Neither would food," Tony said. "It seems like dinner was a long time ago."

"Right, and it didn't exactly sit well when we had to race out of the restaurant."

"And damn Dr. Walker," Tony suddenly exploded. "Why the hell does he always have to be the odd one out, to do something that completely doesn't go along with the rest of us?"

"I think in this case it was fear," Vanessa said quietly. "I can't imagine that he felt comfortable with the circumstances and was looking for a way to get back to some normality. In his world, normality means, *law enforcement officers are the good guys. The militia are the good guys. Government representatives are the good guys.*" She shrugged. "Just think about what he does. It's his regular routine day after day. He's married. He goes to work at a university and comes home to his wife and family."

"His wife must be a saint or plain crazy," Tony muttered.

Vanessa smiled gently and continued, "He's a regular all-American kind of guy. He's not a sports fanatic, but he probably watches various sports on TV. He's not a gamer, probably doesn't even know what that means in today's age. He's a family man. He's a worker, and that's all there is in his life, and he's quite happy with that."

"I guess," Tony said. "It's just frustrating because there's so much else to life."

"Sure, and you're happy to have something else in your life. You've got Franco. And that's great. Dr. Walker has his wife. I think her name is Jenny or something like that." She frowned, trying to recall it. "I can't quite remember. But I think she's a teacher. Something else that would match Dr. Walker's concept of normality perfectly. Not only that, I think she's like a daycare teacher, dealing with young children, or maybe a first-grade teacher or something, working part-time. You know? That whole homemaker thing suits him to a tee."

At that, Tony chuckled. "Let's go see what's downstairs," he said.

They trooped to the kitchen, turned on the little lights over the stove and took a look around to see what there was. With the curtains closed, it shouldn't be obvious that anybody was on board. But they kept the rest of the lights off, just in case.

Scouting through the supplies, they found real food and drinks. Both alcoholic and non. When she found a package of coffee beans, she crowed with delight. "How about you? Are you up for coffee?"

He found the coffeemaker and a grinder and pulled both out so they could use them.

With beans ground and the coffeepot dripping, she settled on a cushioned chair. "This is quite a luxurious sailboat." She looked around. "Most of my water experience has been left to small power boats and the research vessels."

"Mine too," Tony said, sitting across from her, the aroma of coffee filling their small cozy kitchen. "Are you hungry?" He'd found a package of peanuts, some chips and what looked to be pepperoni. They shared the feast. "How long do you think it'll be?"

She shook her head. "Hours," she said soberly. "It's two in the morning now. We probably won't hear from them or see them until at least six."

"Is that an arbitrary assessment?" Tony asked. "You worked that out how?"

"I don't know," she said. "I'm just guessing they would want to be here in the dark though, don't they? So that would mean early morning hours?" She thought about all the guys had to do and then shook her head. "Although no way they'll grab both men and get them back here by six."

"If they need darkness," Tony said, "they might not be back until tonight."

The two exchanged sober looks.

"And that's a scary thought," she said. "I'm much happier here than I am in that dingy hotel room, but it's hard waiting and not knowing what the hell is happening."

Tony nodded. "I hear you. Still, it's what we have, so it's what we'll do."

When the coffee was done, they poured themselves a cup each and sat down to enjoy some more snacking. When she was finally full, she said, "There's no point sitting here. I think I'll go lie down."

"Will you wake if he calls?"

She winced. "Right. So what do we do? Not sleep for the next twenty-four hours?"

Just then the phone rang. Terrified, she stared at it, then snatched it up off the table. "Hello?"

"It's me," Vince said. "We won't make it back before the darkness is gone. We'll be there before noon though, so hold tight. We're coming." And he hung up.

He hung up so fast, she didn't get a chance to ask any questions. She turned to Tony. "He said they'll be here before noon." Vanessa shook her head. "How the hell will they make it back in daylight?"

Tony sighed. "We have to trust. They haven't let us

down yet."

She smiled. "Isn't that the truth? And noon is a long way away." She motioned at the clock beside them. "We can either rest now, which is probably our best bet, or we can sit up and wait some more."

"No point," Tony said. "Let's go check out the sleeping quarters."

There was a bedroom and a bunk room. As they walked into the bedroom, she gave a happy sigh. "Can you imagine if this was actually a holiday? This is ultimate luxury."

The bed was on a pedestal, which probably hid all kinds of storage underneath. Soft lights, when they turned them on, filled the area. They shut them off.

Tony said, "We might be better off if we stay in here together."

"Agreed," she said. "I get the left side of the bed though."

"Blankets on? Blankets off?"

She frowned. "I would sleep better with a blanket on."

"Me too." He pulled the bedspread off the top.

She chuckled, and, with gratitude, she crawled in, laid her head on the pillow.

Tony covered her up, then scrambled in on the opposite side of the bed.

She whispered, "Good night, Tony."

His soft heartfelt whisper came back. "Good night. Sleep tight."

JOHAN WAITED JUST on the other side of the gate for Vince. He'd tied up the canoe, crept alongside the mooring. Johan opened the gate, and they slipped out, relocked it.

As they headed back into the alley, Vince asked, "Any news?"

"Yeah. Looks like they're preparing to move."

"So the eyes you found are working it out?"

Johan nodded. "And he's here with wheels for us."

That would make the job a hell of a lot easier. They bailed into the waiting car, Johan taking the passenger seat in the front, while Vince slid into the back seat. He wasn't sure about the driver. He looked like somebody you would meet in the back alley with double switchblades and who would take your liver faster than you could say, *Hey*. But he and Johan talked calmly.

With no lights, he drove through town, coming to the side of a large estate. Vince hadn't even noticed they'd shifted from low-end to middle-class to high-end houses. He studied the estate and saw it didn't matter where you went around the world, they still looked the same. Like fortresses.

As they watched, the gates opened, and a large black SUV drove out slowly. The driver's phone went off. He checked the text and said, "Both guys were loaded into the back of the SUV."

"How many men are with them?"

The driver sent a text back as he pulled several blocks behind the SUV. "Four."

"That's not good," Vince said. "Means they're prepared to ward off an attack."

Vince agreed. "Any place to take them out?"

"Depends on where they're heading," the driver said. "If it's an exchange to another estate, we need to get them before they get into the other property."

"Is it likely to be that?" Vince asked. "Is there a private airstrip around here? Any small marinas?"

"The airstrip is more likely," Johan said, thinking fast, now dialing his phone, speaking to someone. "Stone is checking for something like that close to us."

Vince could hear half of Johan's conversation as he spoke on the phone. As it was only half, it wasn't helping him to clarify anything. He tried to block it out.

When Johan put down his phone, he turned to Vince and said, "A small airstrip is up ahead, about three miles from here."

Grim, he nodded. "It'll be our only chance."

Johan turned to the driver. "Any chance of weapons?"

The driver cackled. "For money there's always a chance."

"We have money," Johan said in a harsh tone. "And there's a bonus if we get these people back safe and sound."

The driver nodded happily. "Then we can do a deal." He sent off a text and said, "We'll head for the airstrip on the assumption that's where they're going." Then he warned, "But we must be willing to change our plans if they do not turn in that direction."

"Always," Johan said.

In the back seat, Vince struggled to understand what was going on. Why were the guys in suits taking Dr. Walker and Jasper out of the country? And where was that flight going? Being a small airstrip, they were likely to fly under the radar, and nobody would file a flight plan. They could go anywhere in the world.

Levi called Vince just then. "We've got satellite eyes on both of you."

Vince grinned. "Now that's good to hear. Apparently we have weapons being procured."

"Good to know," Levi said with relief in his voice. "That was my next question. No way I can get any help to you in time."

"No," Vince said, "but I would love to know what the hell is behind all this."

"With the Colombia connection," Levi said, "it sounds like Dr. Sanchez is the one behind the original attack."

"Behind it or was the target of it?" Vince asked. "I'm not convinced she wasn't involved."

"No, me neither," Levi said, "but it makes no sense to pick up the other two."

"No," he said, "it doesn't. And we won't know if these two are in on it until we take down the vehicle. Perhaps this is actually a rescue to get these two out of the country. I don't have any way to know. But, considering the black-suited guys' furtive movements and shifting these people in the dark, we must go on the assumption Dr. Walker and Jasper are being taken against their will."

"They certainly haven't managed to get a message out either way."

"Not sure they can," Vince said. "Just so much is going on right now. And they don't have any electronics."

"So watch your back as you go into this play," Levi said. "I'm still not sure we should have left the other two alone on board the boat so near to the bay. The two men who delivered the boat to you originally are still in port. He's getting things set up right now, and he'll head out to the boat to make sure they're okay and stand guard."

"Then I better give her a warning," Vince said. "They won't be too receptive to more strangers showing up."

"Did you give her the other phone?"

"I did. Send her a message for me, will you? Let her know what's going down."

"I'll let her know what's going down in her corner," Levi

said, a note of humor in his voice. "Apparently she can get into trouble if she knows too much."

Vince chuckled. "That is true." Just then the vehicle took a hard right. "Looks like we're heading to the airport," he said.

There was talk on the other end of the phone, then Levi said, "I'm handing you off to Stone now."

There was a short pause.

"Remember. You don't want to get on that plane if you don't have to, and, if we know they're being kidnapped, it's better to take out the plane and stop it from flying."

"Gotcha," Vince said. "Levi doesn't ask for much, does he?"

Stone laughed and hung up.

Johan chuckled from the front seat. "Just everything. He's very much like Bullard. They expect the world and that we'll get it for him."

"The problem is," Vince said, "too often that's exactly what we do. And then they expect more the next time."

The driver nodded sagely. "That is with all bosses. We pull off one amazing feat, and then they want another one and another one. And suddenly, amazing feats aren't enough," he said. "And we have to do more."

Vince chuckled. "Exactly."

Chapter 14

T HE BEEPING PHONE woke her. She snatched it up and
answered it. "Hello? Vince, are you okay?"

"It's not Vince. It's Levi," said the man at the other end.
"First, I've spoken to your father, and he's doing fine. He
knows you're okay."

She closed her eyes and sagged back in the bed. She
rolled over to see Tony staring at her wide-eyed. She held up
a finger and said, "It's Levi."

He relaxed back and listened.

"I'm glad to hear that," she said. "Thanks for contacting
him."

"There's another reason I'm calling. The two men who
delivered the sailboat to Vince and Johan in the harbor,
they're coming to stand guard with you and Tony," he said.
"Dr. Walker and Jasper are being moved again in a black
SUV and are heading for a private airport. Johan and Vince
have gone after them."

"Do we know for sure they've been kidnapped?" she
asked hesitantly. "Has anybody seen if they're tied up or if
they're just part of it all?"

"Interesting thought," Levi said. "I wish I had a con-
firmed answer for you. The fact is, we just know they've
been moved into a vehicle. Two men are in the front of the
vehicle, and two men are on either side of them in the back."

"Protection or guarding?" she asked again.

He chuckled. "I'm glad to see you got your head on straight. But again, I don't have answers. Maybe we'll know as soon as they hit the airport. Johan and Vince will be at the airport probably within an hour. It's five a.m. already where you are. And they've already been alerted that I'm sending the guards on their way to you."

"How are they coming?"

"No idea," Levi said. "I'm sending you visuals, so you know exactly who is coming on board. These are your guards, men from the friend of ours who is lending us your current sleeping quarters."

"And very nice sleeping quarters they are at that," she said with alacrity. She hopped up and looked out the window, surprised to see it was early dawn. "I can't believe it's light out. It seemed like I'd never fall asleep and the night would never end. Then, of course, I crashed, and now it feels like hours have gone by."

"Good," he said. "I hope hours have gone by because, the fact of the matter is, you can do nothing except stay safe. When I get off the phone, remember. I'm sending you two images. Don't let anybody else on board."

She gave a broken laugh. "And just what is it you expect us to do if it isn't these two men?" she cried out. "You realize no weapons are on board."

He hesitated, and then he said, "Actually there are. But, if you don't know how to use them, don't touch them."

The breath whooshed from her chest as she remembered the crates. "I didn't even look last night, but that would explain what Vince grabbed on his way out. He kept it hidden."

"Yes, he would," Levi said. "But remember that's what

he does. He knows how to handle them. He knows how to handle the situation. You don't. So, if it isn't the people you're expecting, send me a message if you can. If not, stay quiet and know Vince and Johan will return." And with that he hung up.

She headed to the kitchen and put on another pot of coffee. She didn't think she'd sleep another wink. As she waited for the machine to drip, two photos came through. Both men looked to be happy-go-lucky sailors. That didn't mean they were though. She'd grown up a lot in the last few days. People weren't who they appeared to be, and she wasn't even sure that Jasper, Dr. Walker or Laura were who she thought they were.

Tony came out and joined her. She filled him in on the little he didn't know. He pointed at the crates and said, "Those are the weapons, aren't they? That must have been what I saw Vince grab on his way out, but I didn't realize what he took."

She said, "I don't even want to look."

"Neither do I, but," his voice turned serious, "it might be our only chance to see if there's something we can handle."

Bolstered by the thought they could have enemies coming their way, and they could get caught again without any way to defend themselves, they lifted the lid off the crates and whistled.

"Wow. Okay. So that's not something I'm prepared to handle."

But the second crate held handguns. Hesitantly she picked one up, and, keeping it pointed to the floor, she said, "Am I more dangerous with this or without it?"

"I don't know," Tony said. "This is one of the times

when I feel like my education is sadly lacking. Here I am, just a researcher, and don't even know how to tell if this damn thing is loaded or not."

"And yet," she said, "if we can't tell if they're loaded from looking at them, that means anybody coming on board can't tell either."

He looked at her and grinned. "Good point." He picked one up and laid it on the table. "Do you want a second one?"

"Hell yes." She snatched up something small and black with a snub nose. "This is a little smaller than the ones you and I have. It'll be easier for me to carry." She glanced at her pants. "But how ..." And then she remembered her vest. She took it out of her backpack, put it on, happy to find the handgun fit into its big pockets.

"Good," Tony said. "Now we both have something." He sniffed the air. "Fresh coffee. Damn, that can turn a situation from being downright ugly to feeling like life is almost doable."

She chuckled. "I agree. I think, while we have the chance, we should also consider food."

They rummaged in the kitchen and pulled out stuff to make sandwiches.

"I can only eat one right now," she said, "but I should fix a second one, in case I need it later. We don't know what'll happen once the guards get here."

"And we have no way to really stop them from doing anything because we won't know if they're good or bad," he said, sighing. "Unless we get close enough to see their faces, and they look like their pictures."

"Let's hope they are the men they're supposed to be, and we'll take it to mean they are good guys," Vanessa said with a little smile. She cut her sandwiches in half, sat down and demolished the first half. Before she got to the end of the second half, she said, "You know something? I think I'll eat my second sandwich."

Tony was right there with her. They plowed through their ham and cheese and every vegetable she could find squished between two slices of bread. With a cup of coffee, they stepped up onto the deck to take a look around.

"It's a stunning morning and a stunning location," she said with a smile. "And how damn sad we're in this situation and can't enjoy it."

"We can enjoy it," he said. "We just have to be aware there'll always be that ugly edge to paradise."

"I guess every paradise has that same ugly edge, doesn't it? It's just we spend an awful lot of our time trying to ignore it."

"Exactly," he said. "It doesn't make it any less beautiful. You know how much I love New York, but it's definitely a big city with all the crime that goes with it."

"In the case of New York," Vanessa said with a laugh, "a little more than everywhere else."

He shrugged. "There are more dangerous cities, but it doesn't change the fact every place has something beautiful and something ugly. It's a matter of trying to live in the beautiful, to be aware of the ugly, but not to let it overwhelm you or to be what directs your actions."

She sat down on a big deck chair, loving the way the boat rocked under her feet. "The good news is, right now nobody's coming toward us. The sun is shining. We have coffee. We have full stomachs, and we're not in black SUVs on our way to some tiny private airport."

"I wish we were on the way to the airport," Tony said quietly, "but not on the way to a small backwoods out-in-the-middle-of-nowhere unregulated airport. Because that's dodgy as hell."

THE AIRPORT WAS up ahead. They pulled off the road, watching as the SUV drove to a small hangar. "This is as close as I can get you," the driver said. "You got your weapons now, but do you need extra manpower?"

Johan nodded. "If you're up for it. The goal is to retrieve the two team members here and get everyone back home safe again."

"And what about the getaway vehicle?" He nodded at the SUV ahead. "Are you planning on keeping their vehicle?"

Johan chuckled. "Nope, it's all yours. We do need to get back to the marina. Our vessel is on the water. That SUV goes to the spoils of the war."

With a big grin of satisfaction, the driver said, "Perfect. That thing is worth a lot of money. I'm in. So is my buddy."

"And where is your buddy?" Vince asked.

He pointed to the hangar. "He's already in position. He got in ahead of us."

"Good," Vince said. "But how?"

"Bike," he said. "Motocross bike. He went cross-country and got here about ten minutes ago, dropping off your special-delivery package that we just picked up."

"Perfect," Johan said. "We need to get them out of the vehicle. The plane hasn't come in yet, and we'll make sure they can't get on it."

They exited the vehicle and crept along the outskirts toward the hangar. As they approached from the back, they were happy to see the hangar had no windows. The black vehicle still sat out front. Nobody had gotten in; nobody had gotten out. Above they could see a flashing light coming in. The sun was just rising and would give the plane enough light to set down without landing strip lights. Something definitely not happening on this small airstrip.

As it slowly came in for its approach, they heard car doors opening, and then somebody saying, "Get up now. No more guff out of you."

And that clinched it for Vince and Johan. Dr. Walker and Jasper were prisoners. Vince sent a text to Levi, pocketed his phone, pulled out his handgun and slipped around the corner. Vince noted the SUV driver on his phone, standing at the side of the vehicle.

Vince heard him say, "We're here. The plane is coming in for a landing." The man hesitated, listening. "Yeah, yeah. We got them. We got the two. Do you have the other one?" He listened again. "Yeah? You finally convinced her? Good. Okay, so it's a clean sweep," he said, pocketing his phone.

When he turned, Vince was on him with a chokehold around his neck. He never made a sound as Vince grabbed him by his pressure points and knocked him out cold. Just to make sure he didn't wake up anytime soon, Vince took the handle of his pistol and hit him once across the temple. The body never jumped.

With one down, he heard a muffled sound behind him. He turned and saw Johan taking out a second one. Johan and Vince exchanged hard grins and then shifted into the shadows. The two prisoners stood in front of the vehicle, flanked by two more suited guys. Jasper leaned against the vehicle for support, as if he'd been beaten and couldn't stand on his own. Dr. Walker looked a lot less polished than the last time Vince had seen him.

The captors spoke and then turned and called out,

"Marco, where are you? The plane is coming in."

On that note, Johan and Vince jumped them.

As Vince stepped out of the way of his targeted guy dropping to the ground, he turned to look at Dr. Walker whose jaw dropped, and he burst into tears.

Vince turned to the young man. "Jasper, how badly hurt are you?"

Jasper blinked, his eyes bloody and puffy. "I'm sore, a couple busted ribs. I don't know how much worse," he said. "I really can't walk much."

"Back into the vehicle," Vince barked.

Johan hopped into the driver's side. "Let's go now."

Jasper needed help to get in. With their driver riding with them, and his buddy taking the other car, they pulled out from the hangar. Just before the plane landed, it shot back up into the air.

Vince grabbed the phone and called Levi's number. "Four hostiles down. Plane is taking off. See if you can track it."

"Eyes in the sky are on it," Stone's voice came through loud, clear and steady. "Condition of the prisoners?"

"Suffering but they're alive," he said. "Jasper might need serious medical care. I don't know yet."

"Get them to the boat if you can. Pull up anchor and get the hell into international waters as fast as possible."

"I heard their driver say something about having these two, and yet, needing to know if they had the third, ... a woman. He said something about a clean sweep."

"Have you got his phone?"

"Yeah. Hang on a sec," Vince shuffled through the phones in his pocket. They'd taken wallets and phones and had left the men where they were. Soon the cops would be called to come and collect them. He got back to Stone. "Here it is, at least it looks like it. Okay, the phone call came in about six minutes ago." He rattled off the number.

"Tracing it now," Stone said. "It's a Colombian number. If they've got Dr. Sanchez, what are the chances they've already moved her out of the country?"

"You still think she's a prisoner?"

"Let me find out from the guys, and I'll call you back." Vince turned, looked at Dr. Walker and Jasper and said, "Okay, we're on our way to the marina. But I need to know what your hosts said about Dr. Sanchez."

Jasper spoke up. "They've got her. It was all about her. They came on board, took her, and were busy telling us how easy they'd taken us down."

"Don't worry about that," Vince said. "The fact of the matter is, we need to confirm she isn't part of this."

Jasper managed to open his good eye, watching him in shock. "Hell no. She's not part of this. I saw her. She was crying and protesting, but they grabbed her, threw her over their shoulder and left with her."

"I have to know for sure," Vince said. "Do you have any doubts about whether she was complicit in this?" He turned his gaze to Dr. Walker.

Dr. Walker shook his head. "No, they made it very clear what they would do to her. She's a prisoner." His voice sounded sad. "Jasper is right. This was a setup to grab her. We were only leverage to make her cooperate."

"And it wasn't her trying to get her freedom and disappearing?"

Dr. Walker shook his head. "No. As far as I understand from what Jasper said, she's barely alive. They beat her badly."

"I know where they're going," Jasper said. "There's a huge estate the family lives on in her home country. They're taking her back there."

"I need all the information you have about it."

Jasper gave him what he could, and Vince passed that information on to Stone. "I don't know if we have locals or someone on the ground in Colombia, or if we need to gather a bigger team, but she has been taken back there."

"I'll see. Levi knows a couple groups down there. It might be a good opportunity for them to get back at somebody they've been trying to hurt for a long time. Dr. Sanchez's family are big drug kingpins. Taking them on won't be easy."

"No," Vince said, pinching the bridge of his nose. "It won't. But my job is to get her and the rest of your team safely out of here, and we're having a hard-enough time doing that."

"I know," Stone said. "I'll contact somebody down there. We need to know if we can get her out. You take care of yourself. Over and out."

Chapter 15

HEARING SOUNDS OF a boat arriving, Vanessa and Tony rushed to the rails. It appeared to be a small powerboat pulling up alongside them.

"Oh, shit," she said, bouncing back and away from sight. But she knew it was likely too late. They'd probably already been spotted.

"Why is it an *Oh, shit?*" Tony asked.

"Because there's more than two," she said. "We were only given facial images of two."

"So they needed a third, somebody to take the boat back." Tony shrugged. "Surely that can't be all bad."

She twisted her hair into a knot nervously. "But it can't be good. Anything that's not what Levi said can't be good."

"I think you're worrying too much," Tony said lazily. "Come on. We're on the sailboat. We've had a great several hours. We've had communication. We know everything is going as planned, and the two men, which I definitely recognized one of them, are here. We're safe and sound."

She wanted to believe him, she really did, but she wasn't sure.

Just then two of the men boarded the boat. With big grins, they walked forward with hands out and shook her hand.

Then the third man came aboard. She took one look at

him, and her heart ran cold. She didn't like him one bit. Maybe it was his eyes. They were dark, small, narrow, a little bit too much space between them. She thought there was a saying about that when it came to horses—those eyes meant the horse was stupid or you couldn't trust them. She'd go with the latter because that was exactly how she felt. There was something off about him.

She bolstered up a smile. "Hi."

The men smiled and introduced themselves. "I'm Shawn, and he's Jared."

She shook their hands again, then she turned to the third man, being up-front and bold as she said, "What's your name?"

He just shrugged and said, "Call me Captain Matt."

She frowned. "But you're not the captain, are you?"

Shawn and Jared shook their heads. "No, he's not. He just gave us a ride over," one said. "We were on shore and needed a quick hop."

She nodded but didn't trust any of them now. She turned to Tony to see him lounging on one of the big deck chairs and frowned at him.

He shrugged and smiled. "It's all good. We need to be here for another few hours, and then hopefully we get to leave." He kept his big smile. He pulled on the back of his deck chair to lie it flat, let his body drop back and closed his eyes. "If anybody is making drinks, I'm all for it." He then yawned. "And, if they're not, I'll have a nap."

She got that he was young and naive, but she didn't have the same sense of trust. Shawn and Jared appeared to be easygoing.

They headed into the cabin, talking about food and coffee. But the third man grabbed another deck chair and sat down beside Tony. It was almost as if he was keeping watch on him, wondering if he would be the most dangerous. Tony had his handgun, the same as she did, but he held it completely casually. Unlike her. The weapon sat heavy against her heart.

She hated those thoughts, and she would blame Vince for putting them in her head because she knew he'd have already analyzed the situation. She didn't like anything about this scenario.

She wandered over to where she could keep an eye on "Captain" Matt, but he appeared to be stretched out lazily beside Tony as he slept.

She crept down below to talk to Shawn and Jared. "Hey, is that guy staying here?" she asked worriedly.

They turned to her, their faces lit up. "That's pretty normal. We're a friendly bunch. Don't you worry."

She shoved her hands in her pocket, stepped out of the way from the stairwell, afraid he'd be up there listening. "He wasn't part of the plan."

"Plan's change," they said. "We haven't had any problems. He's definitely been a help to get us out here," one said, "so don't worry about it. If he becomes a problem, we'll take care of it."

She nodded but still didn't like anything about this. She didn't know if she should stay down here with these two or go up on deck where she could keep an eye on the stranger she had no intention of calling *captain*. She needed to be where she could get a picture of him.

She grabbed a coffee, and, sitting where she could keep an eye on the harbor and all the boats coming and going, she sent a text to Levi, telling him about her concerns. The response she got back wasn't reassuring. **Watch your back.**

What does that mean?

Don't trust any of them now.

Her heart sank. She pocketed her phone and sat back, drinking her coffee. Now her heart pounded, and her nerves were stretched taut. Where the hell was Vince? He should be here.

She hated to say it, but she didn't know where he was, and she desperately wanted to contact him but didn't want to take the chance of disturbing him. If he was skulking around town, having his phone buzz and getting him caught or shot wasn't something she wanted to be responsible for.

She got a text a few minutes later that made her heart lighten. **On the way.**

She took a deep shaky breath and whispered, "Thank God for that."

A voice behind her said, "Hey. You enjoying the morning?"

She stiffened slightly and looked up to see "Captain" Matt smiling at her. She nodded. "Enjoying my coffee. Nothing like the peace and quiet of being on deck alone." She tried not to be snide because she didn't want to piss him off, but, at the same time, she definitely didn't want company.

He just nodded and walked ahead of her slightly. "All quiet in paradise." He gave a hard laugh and kept on walking to the bow of the ship.

She could see him somewhat. He pulled a phone from his pocket and made a call. And that terrified her even more. She texted Levi again. **Message from Vince said he's on his way.**

They should be there soon. Stay calm.

"I wish," she whispered.

She pocketed the phone and decided, as her instincts prodded her, to get up and move. She tried to make it look like she was heading toward the stairs, then ducked around to the back of the ship. There she climbed up one of the ladders used to fix the rigging and just sat by the mast, amid the sail, looking out where she could see everybody. She hated that she was being so suspicious, but she didn't know how else to deal with this.

Matt walked around, talking on the phone up at the front. And then he pocketed his phone, glanced around, checking to see where everybody was. He couldn't find her, frowned, and then walked toward Tony, who was still lying there. He pulled the gun from Tony's hand.

Matt reached down with a hard slam of the butt of the gun to Tony's head. She slapped her hand over her mouth. Tony never even woke—he just slumped to the side. Then, with the gun stashed behind his back, Matt dashed down the stairs.

She pulled out her phone and texted Levi. By now she knew she had to hide, but she didn't know where. Levi asked if she had a photo or could take a picture of him.

No, he's gone down below. Her phone rang. She shut the ringer off once she answered it, hearing Levi talking to her calmly.

"Did you get a good look at him?"

She whispered, grateful the wind was whipping around her. She kept her gaze on the lower cabin to see if he came out. She was half hidden by one of the masts and the billowing sail edge, but it wouldn't be long before he found her.

"He's still down below. But I watched him hit Tony on the side of the head to make sure he didn't wake up. Where the hell is Vince?" she asked in a harsh whisper.

"He's about ten minutes out. Sending him a warning now."

"I don't know where to hide," she cried out, trying not to be overheard.

"Stay where you are," Levi said, his voice calm and steady. He hesitated, then asked, "Do you have a weapon?"

She gave a gurgling laugh. "Have a handgun in my pocket. I don't even know if it's loaded."

Silence.

"I picked it out of the crate. But I don't know how to check it, and I don't know how to use it." She gave a slight groan with her admission. "I was hoping I could bluff my way out of a situation with it."

"Keep it hidden if you can," he said. "You stay hidden too. If you have another place to go that will keep you out of sight, then go and stay there. Just know, Vince is on his way."

She pocketed her phone and huddled against the sail, peering around it to see the cabin.

When the captain, as he liked to be called, came up the stairs, she realized he had already taken care of Shawn and Jared. And now, having searched all the rooms down below, he was looking for her.

She stuffed her fist into her mouth, wishing Vince was only a couple minutes away. She scanned the horizon looking for him. She definitely saw a canoe coming toward them, but it was a ways out. She didn't know what this Matt guy was planning on doing. She just knew she dared not get caught.

She huddled deeper into the sails as the wind picked up, blowing the sails around her. Someone needed to pilot the ship because, if the wind picked up, it would send them way off course. Matt called out, "Hey, Violet or Vanessa, lunch is ready."

She didn't answer.

"You too, Tony," he called out, looking over toward Tony as if thinking he was asleep.

And, if she hadn't seen Matt actually knock Tony out, she would have assumed the same.

He walked around the lower levels, calling for her. He looked over the edge to see if she may have jumped, and then he hopped down into the powerboat he'd brought to see if she'd hidden in there.

All the while Vince stroked strongly toward her. She dared not make a sound. The slamming of her heart should have been loud enough for Matt to hear.

He climbed back up onto the boat. "I don't know where you're hiding, or why you're hiding," he called. "For all I know, you're hurt and fell overboard."

He went from one side to the other. All of a sudden he stopped. He had seen the men in the canoe paddling toward them. She could hear him swear. He dropped down and hid, pulling out a gun. Probably Tony's gun.

She didn't know what to do. Vince and Johan were targets. This man would not give them a chance to get on board and to rescue her. She bit down hard on her lip. She knew she had to do something; she just didn't like the only answer presented to her.

She could see Matt. He was only about twenty or so feet in front of her. She pulled the handgun from her pocket, not even knowing if it would fire. She could see Vince coming closer to their boat. But no way would he see where Matt hid. She saw Matt lining up and putting his sights on the target, probably on Johan because he was in front.

She aligned her own hand with Matt's broad back and whispered a prayer to the wind. Just as he looked like he was ready to shoot, she pulled the trigger. The gun bucked in her hand, sending her tumbling backward. She grabbed for the rigging, almost falling off. She didn't know if she'd hit Matt or something else, or if she had just alerted Vince to the problem. She'd been so surprised that her gun had actually fired that she hadn't realized just what a blowback it would give her.

When she regained her balance, she peered through the sailcloth to see Matt lying on deck. She stared, waiting to see if he would move. She wasn't sure whether he would turn over and shoot her now.

The canoe came up alongside the speedboat, and Johan scrambled from the canoe to the speedboat and onto the boat. He was on top of the gunman in a heartbeat, checking to see if he was alive. He turned him over, checked for a pulse, and then stood and looked in her direction.

She stuck her head around the sail and called out, "Did I kill him?"

He nodded slowly, and she cried out in pain.

And suddenly, Vince was there. He climbed up behind her, his arms wrapping around her. He disengaged the gun from her fingers, tucking it into his waistband at his back, and wrapped his arms around her again.

She threw her arms around his neck and burst into tears.

VINCE COULDN'T BELIEVE when he saw her peeking out through the rigging. He knew Johan had caught sight of her face as he was too good to not be studying what was coming toward them. At the same time, silence was paramount. Sound built upon more sound. So even though they were gliding through the water making the slightest of noises, every noise that added to that amplified it many times over.

He understood that a third man had come on board and possibly had taken out the other two men, hit Tony on the head, leaving Vanessa alone and unprotected. Vince couldn't believe her supposed guards had left her alone to be picked off like that, and it drove power through his arms and into his strokes like never before.

Levi had been very clear about the danger awaiting them, but there was only so much Vince and Johan could do about that. If they were approaching an ambush, then they would get prepared to be ambushed. Vince just had to have a plan in mind when he hit the boat. He hadn't expected to see a gunman lining up his shot. He had expected him to wait until they got on board, when he could have taken them all prisoner. He had that part already worked out.

But, when he'd heard the gunfire and saw the man crumble behind the mast, he realized what had happened. She'd fired a gun and shot somebody. Potentially saved his life or Johan's and, indeed, Tony's.

Vince, still high up the mast with Vanessa, had exchanged a shocked look with Johan on the deck, who had just done a full sweep of the ship. He said, "Taking the speedboat to collect the others."

Vince lifted a hand in response as he held Vanessa in his arms and waited for her tears to subside, which he knew were a reaction to being afraid of so many things—afraid she wouldn't hit the guy, afraid she would hit Vince or Johan. Now upset she had killed him. He understood killing a man was never easy. It shouldn't be easy. There should always be some pain and grief and regret, wondering if there had been another way.

When her crying didn't stop, he squeezed her tight and whispered, "You're fine. It's okay."

Suddenly she reared back, looked up at him and smacked him hard across the face. "It almost wasn't okay," she cried out. "I killed a man. Don't you realize how close he came to shooting you?"

Something warm and silky slid through his heart. He gently wiped the tears from her face. "But he didn't. You saved us."

She stared up at him, a woebegone look on her face. "I killed a man. I've never killed anyone before in my life."

"And I hope you never have to again," he said, "but, as you saw, he was trying to shoot us."

She nodded. "I was so hoping he wouldn't do anything like that because I didn't even know if the gun would fire." She stared at her hand with loathing, as if the gun were still there. "I hate guns."

"You might," he said, "but imagine if you hadn't taken that shot. Imagine if he had shot Johan or me or Tony or all of us. And then he would come after you."

She dropped her forehead against his chest.

He whispered, "Worst-case scenario, he could have shot all four of us. We were all sitting ducks. He could have picked us off one by one. And then you would have been left with just him."

He could feel the shudder rippling up and down her frame. He didn't want to scare her, but he needed her to realize how serious this was. And the fact that what she had done had been necessary. He held her close, and, when he figured it was safe, he tilted her chin up and said, "And, for me, thank you for saving my life." He kissed her gently. He expected her to just half smile and maybe look sad, but instead she flung her arms around his neck and kissed him back passionately.

The heat struck a live chord after his own panic when seeing her hiding up in the top rigging. He'd been so desperate to get to her, and here she was in his arms, kissing him with all she had. He couldn't believe it, and he didn't want to leave her. He wanted her in his arms downstairs in a bed where he could spend time with her, exploring each other, finding out who they were, what they were, and if this was something they both really wanted.

When she finally drew back and cuddled up into his arms, her face against his neck, he felt something soft and tender encapsulate his heart.

He'd been on the road for a long time, hadn't had a long-term relationship in years. His job had made it very difficult to do that. After he left the military and had signed up with Levi, he hadn't expected to find anyone himself. He hadn't been looking. There had been women, many over the years, but nobody he cared about. They'd all known the score, and none had ever lasted. He'd become a little bit of a loner over time, but now? … Now he was completely dumbstruck at the circumstances that had thrown this woman into his arms.

He slowly helped her off the rigging so they now stood on deck. She walked over to where the dead man lay. She bent down, placing her fingers on his neck to make sure he wouldn't get back up. She bowed her head and whispered something. Vince figured it was an apology.

Then she walked back into his arms and just hung on. It wasn't long before he caught sight of Johan, returning with the rest of the team. Finally they'd be all together again. Well, except for Dr. Sanchez. That would take longer.

As the others came on board, she looked at Johan and smiled. "I'm so glad he didn't kill you."

Johan gave her a gentle smile. "I am too."

She walked over to Tony, still on the deck chair, and checked on him. By the time she turned around, she saw Jasper and Dr. Walker sitting on the deck surface. Slowly she walked over to them. She dropped to her knees beside Jasper.

"Oh my, what did they do to you?" she cried out.

"Beat me up pretty good," Jasper said. "They were looking for information that Dr. Sanchez hadn't shared, only I didn't know anything."

"They already had her, didn't they?"

"Yeah," he said, "but they moved her."

"Oh, dear." She turned to Vince. "Any chance of getting her before they take her back to Colombia?"

Vince shook his head, but then his phone rang. He pulled it out, realizing he hadn't updated Levi. "Vanessa's safe," he said boldly with pride. "She shot her captor herself. Stopped him from shooting all of us."

There was shocked silence on the other end, and then Levi laughed. "You know she's a keeper, right?"

Vince frowned. "Don't say that."

"Don't have to," Levi's said. "That's not a term we use anyway. We'll let Mason's group keep that word." He laughed a good long while. "However, it's not over yet. You have to deal with your dead body. Besides, the reason I'm calling is, we've just got word a woman was loaded into a vehicle and was escorted to a yacht somewhere close by you."

"Where from?"

"From your hotel, the first one, oddly enough," Levi

said. "We had men still at the hotel because we were trying to get the rest of your belongings. A small woman was led out, put into a privately owned Land Rover and taken to the docks. They're going to board the yacht named *Princess Marianna*. She can't be too far away from you."

"Do we think it's Dr. Sanchez?"

"We ran through the hotel cameras. We're sending it to you right now, but, as far as we can tell, it's her."

Vince hung up and waited for the photos to come through. When they did, he showed Vanessa. "You recognize her?"

She looked at them and gasped. "That's Laura. She's wearing a scarf, hiding some of her face, but it's definitely her."

He held the phone up to Jasper and Dr. Walker. Both nodded.

"She was taken from our hotel less than thirty minutes ago."

They stared at each other and then back at him.

"Can we help her?" Jasper asked, limping toward Vince. "They are going to take her home and marry her off where her life will be hell from here on in. She tried to leave and have a normal life away from them—and that is not allowed."

Vince studied the big stalwart young man. He was in obvious pain; his face had been badly beaten, and he definitely had some heavy bruising in his rib area. But he was more concerned about Dr. Sanchez. Vince looked at Johan. "According to Levi, she's being driven to the marina and will be on the *Princess Marianna* yacht. Does anybody know anything about that vessel?"

Everybody shook their heads.

Johan disappeared below deck and returned immediately. "Both *guards* are still unconscious."

"Can we wake them up?" Vince asked. "We need answers, and we need answers now."

Johan nodded.

As he went below deck once more, Vanessa turned to look at Vince. "How will you wake them up?"

They heard sounds of splashing water, and then one man roaring.

She raised her eyebrows and said, "Well, I guess that's one way. I guess it's a good thing he didn't just throw them overboard."

Within a few minutes, Vince helped Shawn sit on a deck chair beside the still unconscious Tony, while holding Jared upright, who was slowly waking up, but he wasn't quite as alert as Shawn.

Shawn groaned. "Can't believe we got sucker punched by that guy." He looked over at Vanessa. "I'm sorry. You were right."

She gave him a smart-aleck smirk. "Yeah, you think?"

He had a sheepish look on his face. "I wasn't thinking we would get backstabbed by somebody we know."

"You knew him?"

"Well, we spent a lot of time in the bar with him last night."

Vince groaned. "That's hardly a relationship of trust."

"At a port it is," Shawn said. He put a hand to his head. "But I'll be a long time remembering this one."

Vince figured he probably would. "Do you know anything about the *Princess Marianna*?"

Shawn's eyes lit up. "It's a beautiful yacht," he said. "Comes into port every now and again. Belongs to some fancy rich dude."

"Friendly? Not friendly?"

"I wouldn't say friendly," Shawn said. "The men always have weapons. And you can't ever get on board. My buddy and I tried. We wanted to have a look around, but they weren't letting us on."

"Our Dr. Sanchez appears to have been taken on board." Shawn stared at him. "That is not good. You can't just walk on and get her." He snorted. "Any chance somebody already rescued her, and they're taking her there in order to help her out?"

"It's possible," Johan said. "But, given the scenario, it's not likely. More than likely, two warring drug cartels from Colombia have realized she was here. One would take her home and punish her, and the other would take her back and use her as a weapon against the family."

Vanessa groaned. "So how do we save her?"

"You won't save her," Shawn said. "That's not happening."

"There has to be a way," Vanessa cried out. "We didn't come this far to leave her behind. We've got Jasper and Dr. Walker back. Tony, although he's out cold, he's here, and I'm here. So, we're still missing her."

"I don't know that there'll be a way," Johan said. "We need more men in order to make that happen."

"You need *a lot* more men," Shawn said.

"Unless there's some event or a reason for them to go on shore," Vanessa said quietly. "What kind of diversion can we use to bring them to shore?"

"At the moment she *is* on shore," Johan said, holding the phone against his ear. "Stone's got them on satellite. They're still moored. It looks like they're stocking supplies."

"So we need to hit them now," Vince said quietly.

Johan turned toward the marina. "They're not very far away." He looked at Vince. "How are your swimming skills?"

Vince grinned at him. "I used to work as an undersea diver, and, yeah, I did plenty of military time underwater too."

"Good enough for me," Johan said.

Vince looked over at Shawn. "If I leave you in charge, can we trust you this time?"

Shawn had the decency to look ashamed. "Absolutely." He grinned. "And besides, if I slack off, apparently your girlfriend will take care of business anyway."

Vince watched a flush of pride cross Vanessa's face. He leaned over and kissed her hard. "Isn't that the truth."

She said, "We'll stand watch here."

Chapter 16

PREPARATIONS WERE SIMPLE. They would use the powerboat to head over to the marina and dock along the wharf several boats down. Even if they weren't allowed, they would pick an area, as if they would tie up to an empty yacht, and go underwater, make an entrance onto the *Princess Marianna*, and see if they could take out the men and collect Dr. Sanchez.

It was risky, and Vanessa couldn't believe they were even thinking about it, but Vince acted like it was no big deal. Even Johan laughed and joked. They doubled up on their firepower, both choosing handguns, which somehow they thought were waterproof. Then she watched them put them in plastic.

She didn't even want to watch. She looked out into the ocean, both delighted and hating the fact that poor Laura was there so close, and yet, so far away. She turned to Shawn and said, "How fast can we get out of here once they collect her?"

"I suggest we get closer into port," he said. "We can be within feet of them at that point."

"Good," Johan said. "We've got a good engine here for a fast getaway. Although, if we could disable his yacht that would be better yet. But his engine room will be hard to get to with security on board," Johan said. "Have you any ropes, cables to spare?"

Shawn hopped to his feet, went down below and came back with a long rope. "It's not very heavy-duty, but if you have a use for it ..."

Johan looked at it, nodded, wrapped it around his waist and tied it up.

Vanessa stared at him.

He just grinned and got ready to hop into the power-boat. She stared over at Matt's body. "What do we do with him?"

"Right now, we're not doing anything," Shawn said. "We'll cover him up so nobody can see him, and then we'll have to make a decision. He lived as a river rat. I highly suggest we let him end his life as a river rat."

It was hard to argue with that, but she would struggle with the whole concept of dumping his body overboard. For all she knew, he would sink to the ocean floor, and his family would never know. There would be a mother or a sister or a wife who would never know what happened to him. She struggled with that. "That's hardly fair," she said. "I'm not sure what the better solution is, but I hope we find one."

The men were ready to go. She gave Vince a hard kiss, hugged Johan and said, "Make sure you both get back here."

They hopped into the powerboat.

Shawn said, "I'll turn on the engine and idle this one closer while they take off. We've got the timing down to a split second." He faced Dr. Walker and Jasper. "Both of you go down below. We can't have you seen." He stopped and looked at Tony, still unconscious. "We need to get him below deck too." He picked Tony up and gently carried him below.

Vanessa went to the bow and stood staring forward as

Shawn eased the boat toward the wharfs.

She didn't know how the mooring system worked, but surely they could tie up to an empty one. They needed to find out where Dr. Sanchez was and stay as close as they could.

On that note, she sent a text to Levi. **We're at the marina. Where is the *Princess Marianna*? We're coming in on the sailboat to get as close as we can for the pickup.**

He sent back a GPS location.

She told Shawn, who was piloting the boat.

He nodded. "I know exactly where that is." He shifted directions slightly to come around the end of the wharf.

As they came around, she could see it. "Is that it?" she asked an awe.

He nodded. "It is, indeed. She's a beauty, isn't she?"

She watched as one sentry seemed to walk along the deck on her side. Worried, she chomped on her bottom lip, wondering how close Vince and Johan were. It seemed as if she had glanced away for only a second; then, all of a sudden, there was a splash. She looked back and saw no sentry. She frowned, but Shawn chuckled. "What are you laughing about?"

"Did you see that?"

And she shook her head.

"That was your man. He tossed the sentry overboard."

She watched hopefully, but she never saw Vince.

Shawn pulled up, cut the engine to just idle. They were about twenty feet away.

"Is there a place we can pull in?"

He pointed to a berth. "We can come right up beside them."

And that was what he did. He pulled closer and closer,

and then grabbed the ropes, killed the engine and nudged it forward. She took the rope from him, hopped onto the wharf, and tied it up.

A man from the yacht ran toward them. "Hey, you can't stay here."

Shawn asked him, "Why not?" He pretended to ignore him.

"You can't be so close to the *Marianna*."

"We're just picking up a few people," Shawn said. "We'll be here an hour tops."

The man hesitated, then heard an odd sound. He turned and bolted back toward his yacht.

The *Marianna* rose above Vanessa. It wasn't a superyacht, but, wow, it was gorgeous. She couldn't even imagine how long it was. Eighty feet maybe. It was like a damn house on the water.

She heard the rapid sounds of a gunfight, and then, all of a sudden, there was dead silence. Vanessa looked at Shawn.

He nodded with a finger to his lips. "Pretend to be enjoying the sights. Don't even look at the *Marianna*. Sit there by the rope as if we're waiting for somebody. As soon as you see them coming, you'll unhitch that rope, and we'll pull out of here. You got that?"

"What'll stop them from coming after us?"

"First, we'll make sure none of them are available to come after us," he said calmly. "The second thing is to make sure we're the hell gone from here."

She did as he said, trying not to stare at what was happening beside her. She sat by the rope tied to the dock, nervously wrapping it around a hand and unwrapping it, wrapping it up again, then unwrapping it. Ten minutes passed. Fifteen minutes passed. She kept glancing at Shawn nervously. But he sat on the side with a cigarette and just enjoyed a smoke.

Suddenly came some cheerful whistling, and Johan came up with a couple big bags in his hands. He hopped onto the boat, tossed the bags to Shawn and said, "Are you ready? Let's get this thing fired up."

Shawn hopped over and turned on the engine.

Johan gave her a hand back onto the sailboat, stepped down onto the deck and untied the rope. As he did that, Vince came toward them with his arm wrapped around a woman. She was hunched over, wearing a big poncho. He helped her onto the boat. Vanessa could see it was Dr. Sanchez.

In no way did she show she recognized her, and Vince immediately took her down below. At the same time, Johan pushed the boat away from the dock, the engine already picking up speed as it pulled steadily out and away from the marina.

It hit open water thirty minutes later. She sat on the side, waiting to see if anybody came to join her, not sure if she should go down and see for herself if that was Laura or not. They were powering at a decent speed, putting miles between them and the docks.

When Vince came back up, he went to her side and asked, "Are you okay?"

"I'm scared to hope," she said. "Please tell me that was Laura."

He asked, "Didn't you recognize her?"

She nodded. "I did. I just can't believe it." She opened her arms, and he picked her up, sat down and placed her on his lap.

"It's over."

She shook her head. "No, it can't be over. Not until we're home."

He nodded in understanding. "That's one of the things we were discussing down below. We can still try to make the airport and all your regular flights if you think that's what you want to do. We can go to another marina. It's about ten minutes away. We can grab cabs and head for the airport."

She took a deep breath. "Will they be waiting for us at the airport?"

"The embassy has been alerted, and they're waiting for us at customs."

She'd nodded and said, "Please. Yes. Let's just go."

Thirty minutes later, they stood at customs, clearing their way through. Somehow Levi had managed to get their bags from the hotel, and they were waiting for them as well. They were cleared right through customs. With everybody, including Johan and Vince, boarded, the door to the plane closed behind them as they took their seats.

Vanessa sank down beside Vince. She hadn't even had a chance to say anything to Laura. She could see her with the poncho still wrapped around her, fear and pain on her face.

Jasper was a mess. Dr. Walker had yet to say anything, was so subdued, as if everything in him had been knocked out. Tony was awake and had said something to her, but she'd been so frozen, waiting to see if this would all work out.

But soon the plane taxied down the runway. She knew there was still a huge chance they would be stopped before they lifted up. What they had to do was get in international airspace.

Vince squeezed her fingers and said, "This is where you have to trust Levi."

"Does he have any pull with governments?"

"He's got our government engaged with their government. Believe me. Everybody wants to see us out of here."

At that, a laugh burst free. She squeezed his fingers and said, "So now that we're heading home, where's home for you?"

"I live in Texas. At Levi's compound."

"Right, and, of course, that's near our university. I think I'll stick to research out of Galveston from now on," she said with a laugh.

"No more Galápagos?"

"Not for a while," she said. "Who knows what's in the future? But right now, hell no."

"We'll be landing in another few hours," he said. "Lean back and sleep. I'll make sure you're fine."

And she believed him. "Hey, are you going back home right away?"

"Don't have to," he said. "Why?"

"I was thinking that maybe we started something," she said. "Maybe we need a day or two to figure it out."

He leaned over, his breath warm on her face, and kissed the tip of her nose. "What do you have in mind?"

"I have in mind more than a stolen hour—a weekend at least," she said.

She closed her eyes, curled up, her head on his shoulder. "Wake me when we land."

HE DID THAT. He could see the relief on everybody's faces. But he had meant it when he had said it was in everybody's best interests to have them leave the country. More chaos had ensued than anybody wanted.

As they cleared US customs, Dr. Sanchez lifted the poncho off her head and took several deep breaths. "I'm telling everyone right now. I'm never leaving American soil again."

Vanessa walked over and gave her a gentle hug. "I'm so happy you're alive and well."

With tears in her eyes, Laura whispered, "Thank you so much for saving me."

Vanessa nodded toward Vince and Johan. "It was them," she said. "It was all them."

Taxis awaited them. Dr. Sanchez turned, shook Vince's and Johan's hands and said, "Thank you so very much." She got into the first taxi and took off.

Dr. Walker walked over to Vanessa and said, "I know you don't believe me when I say this, but I'm sorry. I didn't realize what I was bringing down on myself or on you or the rest of the team."

She felt sorry for him. This proud, arrogant man had been humbled by the circumstances. He'd taken a hell of a beating and realized he'd turned in his friends and had brought them even more trouble.

She smiled at him. "Go home to your family, Dr. Walker. It's been a long journey, but we finally made it here at last."

He nodded slowly, got into a cab and headed home.

Jasper and Tony took the next cab. Tony looked at her and asked, "Do you need a ride?"

She shook her head and smiled. "I've already got one, thanks." She turned to look at Johan. "Thank you, Johan. I don't know if you've talked to Vince or not, but I'm kidnapping him for a couple days."

Johan grinned and then chuckled.

Vince just glared at him.

Johan held up his hands and said, "Hey, I've got a Jeep waiting for me. It's a rental, but I'm starting to really like American vehicles. I'll head to the compound. I presume you'll catch Levi up at some point? Or do you want me to do it when I get there?"

"We caught up lots already. I'll see you in a few days." Vince reached out a hand, snagged Vanessa's hand in his. "Do you have wheels here?"

She shook her head. "I took a cab."

"Good," he said, "because my truck is here." They headed to his vehicle. He helped her get in. "Okay, directions?"

Before they were twenty minutes on the road, he pulled up in front of a small brick house. He smiled as he looked at her. "This isn't exactly where I thought you would be living." He hopped out and grabbed their bags.

She exited the truck. "I just rent it," she confessed. "I never cared about putting down roots." A big laugh poured from her. She walked to the front door, unlocked it, stepped inside, dropped the bag she was carrying, waited until he was inside and closed the door behind him.

He dropped his bags here too. They stood for a moment, just looking at each other, then she launched herself at him. He laughed and picked her up in his arms. "Which way?"

"Down the hall on the left," she said, kissing his face frantically. "I can't believe everything we've been through."

"Neither can I," he confessed in between kisses. As she wiggled and moved in his arms, it was all he could do to carry her.

Finally he found the bedroom, walked in, and dropped her on the huge queen-size bed. He fell down on top of her, a lot of his weight on his arms. He lowered his head and kissed her for real. Heat flashed and pleasure seared through him as he captured this woman with so much energy and so much passion and so much vigor. He was blessed to have her for this time. Blessed that he had met her.

"Did all that really happen?" she asked as she pushed on his shoulders until he rolled onto his back. She sat up, straddled him and looked down. "I can't believe these last few days."

And, while he stared up at her in amazement, she unbuttoned her shirt, tossing it onto the chair at the bedside. Sitting in only her jeans and a bra, he felt himself responding to this incredible woman.

"You are something else." He pulled her toward him and kissed her hard.

She wiggled free. "Oh, no you don't. You're wearing way too many clothes."

She hopped off and went to work on his shoes. But she was taking way too long, so he kicked them off, hopped to his feet, stripped down until he stood in front of her completely nude.

And she was too.

He stopped and stared. She was tiny, and yet, so damn curvaceous. Small plump breasts that would fit perfectly into his hand, a tiny waist, beautiful rounded hips.

He shook his head. "Oh, my God, you're beautiful."

She chuckled. "Hell no, I'm not. But, as long as you think so, I'm totally fine with that." She knelt on the bed and opened her arms.

He took her into his embrace, for the first time realizing just how tiny she was. He wanted to be gentle, but she wouldn't have anything to do with it. He wanted to be careful, and she wouldn't let him. He wanted to take his time, and she argued about that.

As she pivoted him onto his back, straddling him once again, she looked down and said, "We'll have time for this all over again soon, but right now I need you inside me."

And, without warning, she lowered herself onto his shaft and plunged until he was seated right at the heart of her. She cried out, his hips lifting until he supported her in the air. Her hands on his ribs held her atop him.

Slowly he groaned at the feeling of being completely sheathed inside her warmth.

She leaned forward and kissed him gently. "It's okay, big guy. I'll be gentle."

He laughed and then groaned again as she started to ride him, her hips lifting and lowering, sliding up and down his shaft, driving him higher and higher. He watched as this Valkyrie—her hair flowing with her every movement, her body moving rhythmically to a musical sequence in her head—pounded herself up and down him.

He grabbed her hips and lunged harder and harder inside. She cried out again, her body arching as she reached her climax. He groaned and lifted and plunged with the thrust of his hips until finally his own body exploded beneath her.

She collapsed, and, after a moment, she chuckled.

He was too exhausted to do anything but gaze at the ceiling and wonder what the hell had just happened.

She smiled and said, "Well, I'm ready for round two. How about you?" She lifted her head until her hands were crossed on his chest and stared down at him.

He stroked her hair off her face and said, "You'll have to give me a minute."

Immediately she counted down the seconds.

He burst out laughing. "Are you always this energetic in bed?"

She shrugged. "Why not? Sex is fun."

He nodded. "It is, indeed."

"But this isn't just sex," she said, slowly sitting up. He was still deeply embedded inside. "This is something else instead."

"What is this?" he asked.

"This is the start of something special."

"Oh, is it?"

She nodded. "Yep. You see? I've come close to death several times, and I've killed a man. I have friends who were beaten and tortured, and a woman I admire deeply was kidnapped because of some power play. It makes you reassess your view on life."

He stared up at her, his hands gliding along her hips up to her ribs to cup her breasts. "In what way does it change you?"

"Makes me appreciate this more." Her fingers slid over his lips, gently stroking his cheeks. "It makes me realize what I'm missing. And, when I find something I want, that I don't make the same mistake everybody else is making and lose it. I don't want to lose something like this because I didn't tend to it, because I didn't water it, because I didn't feed it, because I didn't help it and nurture it so it would grow."

"*This?*" he asked, a smile in his voice.

She kissed his lips, first the bottom one, then the top one, the corners and his nose. "*This,*" she said. "*Us.* I don't know what we have. I don't know where we'll go. But I'm willing to take that step to find out. What about you?"

He smiled, reached down and held her hips firmly. "I'm here, aren't I?"

"Yes," she said hesitantly. "But it would be very hard if this is all you wanted."

"I'm not a one-night-stand type of guy," he said gently. "When I find somebody as special as you, ... I know it. I might not have seen it the first day, but it didn't take me long to wake up and to realize what was happening."

"Are you sure?"

He nodded and smiled. "I'm also sure of something else."

"And what's that?" she asked.

"You talk too much," he said with a chuckle, and he lifted his hips, plunging his ready erection deep inside her again.

She gasped and cried out as her body responded. Her nipples peaked, and a warm flush rolled over her face as passion once again seared through her. "You're right," she said on a groan. "We have much better things to do. We can talk later."

"We can talk now too," he said, "but I'd much rather enjoy what we have. There will be time for talking afterward."

"There will be time for this too later," she said on a laugh, then moaned. "Oh, dear God. I hope there will be."

"I have no intention of stopping this," he said. "Making love with you is something I don't ever see me growing tired of."

"Me neither," she whispered, her back arching once again. "Now you need to stop talking too."

He flipped suddenly, so she lay underneath him, her thighs wrapped around his hips, and he took control. Sending her flying off the cliff once more.

When he followed her a short time later, she gasped and held him close. "Oh, my God."

"Absolutely," he said. "What we have is special."

"No," she said. "You're special."

He kissed her deep, long and hard. "What we have, you and me, we will nurture so we can have it for a long, long time."

She'd never heard anything so sweet in her life.

Epilogue

CELITE DANNING SPUN on her heels and walked away from Levi. It was the hardest damn thing she'd ever done. But she was getting better at it.

He reached out, grabbed her arm, and spun her around again, his face twisted with anger. "What do you mean, *no?*" he roared. "I asked you to marry me, and, anytime I try to set a date, you keep pushing it off. Why?"

Ice stood firm, her hands on her hips. "You're not ready," she snapped.

"It's not for you to tell me when I'm ready or not," he said, his voice gentle as he stared at her searchingly.

She smiled up at him. "No, it isn't," she said, "but it's a momentous time. And I don't want you to make a mistake."

His eyebrows shot up at that. He crossed his arms and said, "Really? You're telling me that I don't know what I want?"

"*Really?*" she said, mimicking him. "Of course, you don't know what you want. You're a man." She laughed and laughed.

He reached out, snagged her up, and kissed her hard. Immediately passion swept over them, as it always did. He held her close, murmuring against her ear. "Ever since I asked you," he said, "I've been trying to set a date. Please put me out of my misery."

"Okay," she said, "but I want to think about it. An awful lot of people are here, and we're likely to start something."

He winced at that but bravely said, "Maybe we should do a group wedding then."

She shook her head. "I don't think that'll work too well. We only got caught up in the last one because of other people's plans," she said. "That's not exactly something we can do here."

"Maybe that's a good thing," he said. "I have to admit that I was a little concerned about that."

She chuckled. "I'm sure you were," she said. "But the bottom line is, that's not exactly a good idea for us."

"So what do you want to do?"

She frowned. "I know Bailey and Alfred will want to do the cooking. I don't want anybody else here but family and friends. I want my father to give me away."

"What about Bullard?"

She stared up at Levi. "I would love that," she said, "but I don't know if you would."

He gave her that lazy, sexy smile that she absolutely adored and said, "Sweetheart, I don't mind in the least. But I don't know if Bullard would want to. Or even has the time to."

"Then we'll leave it to Bullard to decide," she said. "He's a very good friend, as are many of his people. I wouldn't want to exclude them either."

"In that case, you just doubled the numbers here."

She scrunched up her face and shuddered.

He leaned closer and said, "Maybe *you're* the one who's getting cold feet."

Heat flashed between them again, and she shook her head. "No cold feet here," she said. "I can think of nothing I want more than to be your wife."

At that, he kissed her again, but, just as they deepened their kiss, the alarm sounded throughout the compound. They broke apart, stared at each other in shock, and bolted in different directions. Ice headed for the control room, and Levi headed downstairs.

In the control room, Stone already watched the cameras. She stepped inside, and he said, "Lock the door behind you."

Immediately, she closed and locked it and hit the security button. "What's going on?"

"I'm not sure," he said, "but I counted two gunmen with semiautomatic rifles on the top cliff."

She gasped and sat down. The sirens were still going on outside. The pool had just opened. Likely half-a-dozen people were out there, but everybody had been briefed on the alarms. At first sound, everybody must be inside and locked down. It also meant all residents of the compound, all the men and their partners, should be armed and ready for full-on warfare. She hated the fact that she had to live in a war zone, but it was what it was.

And she'd rather live in *this* war zone than continue the work she used to do in a different one. She counted on everybody here to do their job. No way she would let something like this stop her from taking the next step in her life.

"There." Stone tapped one of the monitors. She glanced at it just in time to see a flash from a scope.

She nodded. "Let me talk to Levi."

"He's on the PA system now," Stone said.

"Levi, he's onscreen. We've got one shooter on the back quarter atop the ridge. Rear camera is still working. He doesn't appear to know. We have a second shooter outside our secret door."

"Okay," Levi said, his voice calm and controlled. "Two teams of men will go out. My team'll take the secret door, and we've got another team going out through the back."

"Anybody going out the back is likely to get picked off by the sniper on the ridge," Stone said.

"Maybe," Levi said, "but not if we get there first. We need to come up with another way to get on the other side of that hill without having to go around."

"You want to get a bore in and start tunneling through there?" Ice asked.

"Talk about money," Levi said.

"I don't care," Ice said. "I don't want anything to compromise our security."

"We'll discuss it afterward," he said. "Make sure everybody is accounted for. Do a full roll call, and anybody who's off-base needs to be told that they can't come home."

"Will do," Ice said. It was standard procedure. All the women had been thoroughly briefed before they moved into the compound, but they hadn't had an incident in months—just another reason why they had practice sessions. To keep everybody up to date with safety procedures.

For shit that eventually happened—like now.

This concludes Book 19 of Heroes for Hire: Vince's Vixen.

Read about Ice's Icing: Heroes for Hire, Book 20

Heroes for Hire: Ice's Icing (Book #20)

This is #20 of the Heroes for Hire series!

Ice wanted only one thing in her life, and that was Levi—and maybe someone who was a blend of both of them. When he asked her to marry him, she was thrilled, but now she's struggling to pin down a wedding date for fear he'd been caught up in the moment and didn't really want to go through with it. When the compound is attacked, and they are forced to go on the offense, she realizes what's truly important.

Levi is infuriated that Ice refuses to set a wedding date. He's always loved her, and there will never be anyone else for him. This fact is reinforced as they come under attack by a military group trying to overthrow a government that he aided.

As the bullets fly and the body count mounts, who says you can't have your cake and your icing too!

Ice wanted only one thing in her life, and that was Levi—and maybe someone who was a blend of both of them. When he asked her to marry him, she was thrilled, but now she's struggling to pin down a wedding date for fear he'd been caught up in the moment and didn't really want to go through with it. When the compound is attacked, and they are forced to go on the offense, she realizes what's truly important.

Levi is infuriated that Ice refuses to set a wedding date. He's always loved her, and there will never be anyone else for him. This fact is reinforced as they come under attack by a military group trying to overthrow a government that he aided.

As the bullets fly and the body count mounts, who says you can't have your cake and your icing too!

Book 20 is available now!

To find out more visit Dale Mayer's website.

http://smarturl.it/DMIceIcingUniversal

Author's Note

Thank you for reading Vince's Vixen: Heroes for Hire, Book 19! If you enjoyed the book, please take a moment and leave a short review.

Dear reader,

I love to hear from readers, and you can contact me at my website: www.dalemayer.com or at my Facebook author page. To be informed of new releases and special offers, sign up for my newsletter or follow me on BookBub. And if you are interested in joining Dale Mayer's Reader Group, here is the Facebook sign up page.
facebook.com/groups/402384989872660

Cheers,
Dale Mayer

Your THREE Free Books Are Waiting!

Grab your copy of SEALs of Honor Books 1 – 3 for free!

Meet Mason, Hawk and Dane. *Brave, badass warriors who serve their country with honor and love their women to the limits of life and death.*

DOWNLOAD your copy right now! Just tell me where to send it.

www.smarturl.it/DaleHonorFreeBundle

About the Author

Dale Mayer is a USA Today bestselling author best known for her Psychic Visions and Family Blood Ties series. Her contemporary romances are raw and full of passion and emotion (Second Chances, SKIN), her thrillers will keep you guessing (By Death series), and her romantic comedies will keep you giggling (It's a Dog's Life and Charmin Marvin Romantic Comedy series).

She honors the stories that come to her – and some of them are crazy and break all the rules and cross multiple genres!

To go with her fiction, she also writes nonfiction in many different fields with books available on resume writing, companion gardening and the US mortgage system. She has recently published her Career Essentials Series. All her books are available in print and ebook format.

Connect with Dale Mayer Online

Dale's Website – www.dalemayer.com

Twitter – @DaleMayer

Facebook – dalemayer.com/fb

BookBub – bookbub.com/authors/dale-mayer

Also by Dale Mayer

Published Adult Books:

Hathaway House
Aaron, Book 1
Brock, Book 2
Cole, Book 3
Denton, Book 4
Elliot, Book 5
Finn, Book 6

The K9 Files
Ethan, Book 1
Pierce, Book 2
Zane, Book 3
Blaze, Book 4
Lucas, Book 5
Parker, Book 6
Carter, Book 7

Lovely Lethal Gardens
Arsenic in the Azaleas, Book 1
Bones in the Begonias, Book 2
Corpse in the Carnations, Book 3
Daggers in the Dahlias, Book 4

Evidence in the Echinacea, Book 5

Footprints in the Ferns, Book 6

Gun in the Gardenias, Book 7

Psychic Vision Series

Tuesday's Child

Hide 'n Go Seek

Maddy's Floor

Garden of Sorrow

Knock Knock...

Rare Find

Eyes to the Soul

Now You See Her

Shattered

Into the Abyss

Seeds of Malice

Eye of the Falcon

Itsy-Bitsy Spider

Unmasked

Deep Beneath

From the Ashes

Psychic Visions Books 1–3

Psychic Visions Books 4–6

Psychic Visions Books 7–9

By Death Series

Touched by Death

Haunted by Death

Chilled by Death

By Death Books 1–3

Broken Protocols – Romantic Comedy Series
Cat's Meow
Cat's Pajamas
Cat's Cradle
Cat's Claus
Broken Protocols 1-4

Broken and... Mending
Skin
Scars
Scales (of Justice)
Broken but... Mending 1-3

Glory
Genesis
Tori
Celeste
Glory Trilogy

Biker Blues
Morgan: Biker Blues, Volume 1
Cash: Biker Blues, Volume 2

SEALs of Honor
Mason: SEALs of Honor, Book 1
Hawk: SEALs of Honor, Book 2
Dane: SEALs of Honor, Book 3
Swede: SEALs of Honor, Book 4

Heroes for Hire

SEALs of Steel

Laszlo: SEALs of Steel, Book 5

Geir: SEALs of Steel, Book 6

Jager: SEALs of Steel, Book 7

The Final Reveal: SEALs of Steel, Book 8

SEALs of Steel, Books 1–4

SEALs of Steel, Books 5–8

SEALs of Steel, Books 1–8

Collections

Dare to Be You…

Dare to Love…

Dare to be Strong…

RomanceX3

Standalone Novellas

It's a Dog's Life

Riana's Revenge

Second Chances

Published Young Adult Books:

Family Blood Ties Series

Vampire in Denial

Vampire in Distress

Vampire in Design

Vampire in Deceit

Vampire in Defiance

Vampire in Conflict

Vampire in Chaos

Vampire in Crisis

Vampire in Control

Vampire in Charge

Family Blood Ties Set 1–3

Family Blood Ties Set 1–5

Family Blood Ties Set 4–6

Family Blood Ties Set 7–9

Sian's Solution, A Family Blood Ties Series Prequel Novelette

Design series

Dangerous Designs

Deadly Designs

Darkest Designs

Design Series Trilogy

Standalone

In Cassie's Corner

Gem Stone (a Gemma Stone Mystery)

Time Thieves

Published Non-Fiction Books:

Career Essentials

Career Essentials: The Résumé

Career Essentials: The Cover Letter

Career Essentials: The Interview

Career Essentials: 3 in 1